"I've Been Through This Heartbreak,"

Clementine told Evan. "When the person you cherish decides to choose another. Time will heal...."

Clementine withdrew her hand from Evan's arm, because if ever a man looked like he didn't want consolation or touching or hugging, it was Evan Tanner. She'd seen a stray dog bristling like that once, wounded and ready to snap at anyone comforting him.

Evan's sudden coldness was probably based on his *problem,* she decided. "You can cry if you want to," she offered softly.

He stared at her blankly. "Cry?"

Clementine stepped closer....

Dear Reader,

This month it seems like everyone's in romantic trouble. We have runaway brides and jilted grooms....They've been left at the altar and wonder if they'll *ever* find true love with the right person.

Of course they do, and we get to find out how, as we read Silhouette Desire's delightful month of "Jilted!" heroes and heroines.

And what better way to start this special month than with *The Accidental Bridegroom,* a second 1994 *Man of the Month* from one of your favorites, Ann Major? I'm sure you'll enjoy this passionate story of seduction and supposed betrayal as much as I do.

And look for five more fabulous books by some of your most beloved writers: Dixie Browning, Cait London, Raye Morgan, Jennifer Greene and Cathie Linz. Yes, their characters might have been left at the altar...but they don't stay single for long!

So don't pick and choose—read about them all! I loved these stories, and I'm sure you will, too.

Lucia Macro
Senior Editor

Please address questions and book requests to:
Silhouette Reader Service
U.S.: 3010 Walden Ave., P.O. Box 1325, Buffalo, NY 14269
Canadian: P.O. Box 609, Fort Erie, Ont. L2A 5X3

CAIT LONDON
THE BRIDE SAYS NO

SILHOUETTE *Desire*®
Published by Silhouette Books
America's Publisher of Contemporary Romance

SILHOUETTE BOOKS

ISBN 0-373-05891-8

THE BRIDE SAYS NO

Copyright © 1994 by Lois Kleinsasser

Books by Cait London

Silhouette Desire

The Loving Season #502
Angel vs. MacLean #593
The Pendragon Virus #611
The Daddy Candidate #641
Midnight Rider #726
The Cowboy #763
Maybe No, Maybe Yes #782
The Seduction of Jake Tallman #811
Fusion #871
The Bride Says No #891

Silhouette Books

Spring Fancy 1994
"Lightfoot and Loving"

CAIT LONDON

lives in the Missouri Ozarks but grew up in Washington and still loves craggy mountains and the Pacific coast. She's a history buff and an avid reader who knows her way around computers. She grew up painting landscapes and wildlife, but is now committed to writing and enjoying her three creative daughters. Cait has big plans for her future—learning to fish, taking short trips for research and meeting people. She also writes as Cait Logan and won the *Romantic Times* Best New Romance Writer award when she first started writing.

To Gavin Thomas Davis, born 12/8/93 to Lana and Tom Davis.
To Melissa Senate, my honey of an editor, whose continued TLC is very appreciated.

One

He's already sexually dysfunctional. Getting jilted by my sister certainly won't help, Clementine thought as the cowboy's dark, work-hardened hands opened the envelope she had just handed him.

As he read the note, Evan Tanner loomed over her, his black western hat tugged low on his head, the brim dusted with snow. A delicate snowflake fluttered to his darkly tanned skin, rolling across his lean cheeks and lodging in the straight raven hair behind his ear. His mouth tightened and Clementine sensed that he rarely smiled. A westerner standing in front of two saddled horses and a mule, Evan Tanner suited the rugged mountains of north-central Washington State. The late-March snow clung to the worn shearling coat covering his broad shoulders and flowed between his locked-at-the-knee legs to cover his scarred western boots. The small frayed holes on his faded jeans lent to his down-on-his-luck appearance, which caused Clementine's heart to ache. Her sister's note looked fragile in his big hands.

She reached to dust away the snow from the note that would rip his poor wounded heart to shreds; Claudia had decided to break their engagement—Evan had been jilted, the second Tanner man to be jilted by a Barlow woman. The first event had set off a feud that had lasted three generations.

Evan glanced at her impatiently and Clementine's fingers ached to soothe away the deep furrow between his slashing black eyebrows.

At thirty-six, Clementine understood the pain of a broken heart—she'd been divorced, then with a new love she'd stood in front of the altar only to be handed a note much like Claudia's.

Two years ago, Morris had insisted on a costly, magnificent wedding to meet his "social set's standards." That was before he decided to elope with someone else, leaving Clementine at the altar in her French lace gown. The unfinished affair took all her savings, but when she recovered—and made payments on the baker's and the caterer's outstanding bills—she realized that marriage to Morris would have been endless and empty.

Yet at the time, standing in her bridal gown and crushing her huge bouquet of roses and baby's breath—which had probably come from this same Okanogan Valley area—against her lace-covered bosom, Clementine had been shattered. She'd barely managed the lengthy bridal train that Morris had insisted upon as she walked back down the aisle, forcing a smile for her family and friends. Later, she wondered how she had ever managed to invite the four hundred guests to the wedding buffet, which Morris also had wanted for his social peers.

Most of the guests had escaped the fiasco quickly and she'd eaten a stack of limp and soggy watercress sandwiches. She had frozen a year's supply of sweet-and-sour drummies—the upper part of the chicken wing. The clam chowder that was to have been served in crusty sourdough bread bowls had been frozen in jars. She couldn't bear to eat one more cup of clam chowder.

Then her father and Evan's senior partner, Jack Barlow, had passed away as he had lived, playing cards and smoking a cigar, and another grief had washed away the first.

She hoped the lean, tall cowboy standing in front of her would be able to show his grief, which was emotionally better for him.

Evan Tanner had enough scars.

She had come to rescue him, in addition to her personal reasons. One of which was that she had nowhere else to go.

Evan's gray eyes flicked over Claudia's round, even script, which announced her marriage plans for November. The taut cord crossing his jaw and flowing into his muscular throat tensed, his black eyebrows slashing together. Another snowflake caught on his sweeping lashes and fluttered onto a nose that was straight, blunt and masculine. A lacy, fat flake caught on the dark stubble covering his jaw. His lips tightened again before his eyes slashed down at Clementine.

She sensed that Evan's pioneer and Native American ancestors had likely slashed that same arrogant look down at other women. There was an all-male, rugged challenge to Evan's dark, impatient look, as if he didn't like feminine intrusion.

Clementine trembled just once. She was invading Evan's kingdom—the Barlow Guest Ranch.

Besides sharing duties in the venture, she planned to tend Evan's psychological wounds.

He didn't look very receptive right now. The muscle contracting in his jaw was not encouraging, nor the rigid set of his broad shoulders blocking the icy wind from her. He looked intimidating, frustrated and impatient.

She refused to straighten her navy beret, a cocky little investment that suited her rebellious mood since she'd decided to move from Seattle. Clementine had based her decision on two major events—inheriting her father's senior partnership in Evan's guest ranch project and getting dismissed at the marriage altar. With a divorce and a broken engagement behind her and a boring future lurking ahead, she'd decided to sell her investment in the small florist shop she owned and strike off on new horizons. As Evan's working partner, she could salvage her pride, build a nest egg and be creative. The whole idea—Evan Tanner's idea—of rebuilding an 1880s gold- and silver-rush town for wealthy patrons excited Clementine. The previous first summer of business had proven that the concept had possibilities when wealthy businessmen vacationed and "roughed" it at the old hotel.

While Evan had worked in construction all over the world and was a great carpenter, Clementine also had skills that would lend to the guest ranch idea. Though she was the senior executive in the venture, she intended to work as his partner. She visualized them as two people combining ideas for success—

Evan's smoky eyes drifted to her lips and her thoughts slammed to a stop. Clementine decided she was overexcited and tired; she licked her lips with the tip of her tongue. No doubt Evan would see the opportunities of expanding the men-only "roughing-it" vacation site to offer adventures in gold panning and ranching for women. Then there was always herbal gardening and weaving.

The incredible, fascinating idea of structuring a business that could be profitable and fun was too good to dismiss. The mountains in Washington State's Okanogan Valley were filled with small boom towns like Loomis and Conconully and Ruby that had faded away. Evidence of gold and silver mining remained, lodged in the craggy mountains covered with pine trees, rocks, sagebrush and sand. The countryside was perfect for the "rough-it" crowd. With all these possibilities gleaming like a miner's gold nuggets, Clementine had invested her savings in buying out Claudia's portion of Jack Barlow's estate.

Clementine touched her jaunty little beret and straightened her shoulders. The icy northern wind nudged a swathe of shoulder-length, nut-brown hair across her cheek and she pushed it behind her ear. She hoped Evan's steely gaze missed her last shiver as a dollop of snow slid down her new red western boots. She shivered again as he looked down the long, dressy maxicoat, her brand-new jeans and boots. His gray eyes slowly rose to lash contempt on her beret. She ignored the visual sneer. The perky little cap was her statement; she'd changed the course of her life, making a fresh start.

"While my father owned the land and was a silent partner, I favor a hands-on approach. I'm here to help you make the project a success. I'll work very hard to help you," she corrected because the idea had been Evan's, while her father had supplied the funds.

"The little do-gooder," Evan said tightly, thoughtfully, his cold eyes boring into her. "Is Claudia happy?" he demanded.

Clementine shivered again. Evan was upset; he had repeated Claudia's nickname for her. Just for a moment, she wanted to step back into the rental van with her belongings. Evan's gaze slashed to the front end of the van, which was buried in the three-foot snowdrift created by Tex Murphy's truck plow, then back to her. Clementine hoped that the man who would return the van wouldn't mind digging a bit.

"I said, Is Claudia happy?" Evan asked softly, biting off the words.

"Very. Evan, she wants more than a marriage of Barlow and Tanner lands," Clementine returned slowly, lifting her face. The demand in Evan's deep, raspy voice raised the hair on the back of her neck. She refused to be intimidated by Evan Tanner, though she understood his curt manner—"He'd ridden a bad luck horse most of his life," according to her father. She blew a snowflake away from her lips and decided that she might as well open Claudia's decision not to marry Evan Tanner to the freezing, morning winds. "She wants more than a father to her sons," she said as gently as she could.

"At nine and eleven, boys need a father," Evan snapped, looking as unmovable as the mountains behind him. He flicked an impatient glance at her gleaming red boots.

Clementine knew his heart was breaking, his dissolved dreams pouring down around his long, denim-covered, wide-spread legs. She chose not to step into the area of Claudia's full-blown need for sensuality and Evan's inability to fulfill her intimate needs. Claudia had chosen Richard, a romantic, open, friendly man, over Evan, who now stood before Clementine like a man of stone. As if he'd eaten the worst of life's smorgasbord buffet. "She loves Richard," she said gently.

"Love," he repeated hollowly and Clementine's heart tore slightly, aching for him. Claudia had said that Evan

Tanner had seen little enough of it after his parents divorced. When his mother died, he had been tossed into the hands of his bitter, alcoholic father, then into several foster homes. At nineteen, Evan had married a girl his age and had to battle her wealthy parents every inch. The marriage had ended in disaster when he discovered his wife with another man, one her parents had picked as his successor.

He rubbed the stub of his right thumb across his jaw and the thoughtful gesture drew Clementine's gaze. According to Claudia, Evan had lost that thumb in a rodeo calf-roping competition. He was just fourteen, supporting himself and his dying father, but he had continued and won the prize money. Evan's infrequent, brotherly kisses and the fact that he had not tried to make love to Claudia led the sisters to believe that rodeo bronc and bull riding might have injured him and taken away his desire. With Clementine's amateur psychology interpretations, Claudia had decided that Evan's stormy teenage marriage might have added additional trauma, rendering him sexually dysfunctional. Claudia's answers to the questionnaires in Clementine's magazines had also proven that Evan might not be highly sexual.

Clementine's heart lurched as Evan looked off into the pine trees studding the rugged mountains. He jerked on his leather gloves. "I've been close to those boys for two years since her husband died. I liked Claudia and I liked those boys. I would have taken good care of them—I wanted to take care of them and give them a good solid home... to protect them and Claudia. A soft woman like her could get hurt—"

Clementine thought of the sexual sparks flying between Claudia and Richard and ached for Evan. With his problem, it was unlikely that he could understand the heat and fire that Claudia and Richard shared. Even without their sexual attraction, they would still have love, a commodity Evan had not offered.

The cord crossing his cheek tightened as he paused, then continued with a savage tone ripping under his deep, soft voice, "We had a good, strong understanding. A Tanner marrying a Barlow would reunite the land. The boys would have grown up on land that had been passed down since homesteading days. That's important—providing the boys with a sense of belonging. Do you think her . . . her fiancé will be good to them?"

Clementine remembered Claudia's worried reference to Evan's troubled life—he was just five years old when his parents divorced and the Tanner land fell into ruin and bankruptcy. The Barlows bought the property, which deepened the breach in the long-term homesteading families. She placed her hand on Evan's arm. "Land is important. But so is Claudia's happiness. Richard is a kind man. . . . It's for the best, you know," she said quietly. "I've been through this—heartbreak, when the person you cherish decides to choose another— It's really for the best, you know. . . . Time will heal—"

His eyes lashed down to her mitten-covered hand, then at her face. She withdrew her hand because if ever a man looked as though he didn't want consolation or touching or hugging, it was Evan Tanner. She'd seen a stray dog bristling like that once, wounded and ready to snap at anyone comforting him. Jimbo had grown to be a huge cuddly monster basking in her hugs and kisses and had passed away at a ripe old age.

Evan's freezing aura was probably based on his sexual dysfunction, she decided. When Clementine jammed her hand into her coat pocket, her fingers burned with the feel of Evan's unrelenting strength. "You can cry if you want to," she offered softly.

He stared at her blankly, then shook his head as if zooming in from another galaxy. "Cry?"

Clementine stepped close to him, hugged him and tugged his head down for a kiss on his cheek. She sensed the slightest resistance before he allowed her to draw him down to her level. The stubble on his cheek scratched her lips slightly; he smelled of leather and wood smoke and a darker, headier texture that sent tingles swirling around her senses like tiny, twinkling Christmas-tree lights. She pushed away the fragile link between a Merry Christmas and the rugged cowboy. Perhaps Christmas had leapt into her mind because she had recently stored her holiday ornaments. She stepped back and looked up at him worriedly. "It's better to show emotions, rather than to bury them. Men do cry nowadays. I won't mind," she whispered gently, handing him a neatly ironed flowery handkerchief.

His eyes, the color of smoke riding a night sky, held her as he ignored the offer of crying and the handkerchief. A vein thudded heavily in his temple; his mouth tightened ominously.

"Are you sure you want to do this?" he asked tightly.

She'd left one world for another and a new life. "Yes," she said firmly. "I want this."

"Uh-huh," he said flatly. "You're not ruining what I've built. And you won't last."

"We'll have to see about that, won't we?" she asked, surprised by the riffle of anger aroused by his challenge. "I have every intention of making our project a success."

"Our project," he repeated in that disbelieving flat tone. "Lady, I've worked night and day for two years to

get this ranch-for-wealthy-backsides-idea off the ground.
Your father supplied the land—Tanner land. My life savings are invested in an idea *I developed.*"

Clementine met his hard stare. Her fist crumpled the paper in her pocket, the magazine article on choosing a perfect lover. Clementine based a certain amount of her decisions on magazine questionnaires. She'd wished she had started taking quizzes on potential life mates before saying yes to Morris.

Looming over her now, Evan's jawline locked in a stubborn clench. He did not suit the latest questionnaire she had filled out—"Profile of a Lover." She couldn't see him in romantic foreplay. There was nothing tender and friendly and sensitive about him. She could be just as stubborn. "My life savings are invested in the development, too. So, we'll just have to make a go of it, won't we?"

His smile didn't reach his eyes. It reminded her of a wolf baring his teeth and waiting for his prey to enter his trap. He nodded to the van. "Is that everything?"

She touched her beret and straightened her shoulders. "Those are just my necessities. The movers will be here in another month."

Evan allowed Yuma, his Appaloosa stallion, to pick his way around the stands of snow-laden sumac bushes and pine trees. Familiar with the winding, treacherous, snow-covered trail that led from Loomis to Evan's ghost town—formerly the Bliss Hotel and Saloon—Yuma nickered and Mosey, the aged mule, brayed.

The usual one-hour trip would take longer because of the trail's poor mud and snow conditions.

Evan glanced over his shoulder past the heavily laden mule to the woman—Claudia's agile little do-gooder sister, seated on Belle, an Appaloosa mare. Unprepared for the freezing temperatures, Clementine clutched the horse's saddlehorn with one hand. She huddled beneath the blanket he had tucked around her and protectively hugged a huge, leafy plant against her. She'd refused to leave the plant to "freeze to death," and had gathered it lovingly to her body. She had received the plant from a dying friend and had promised to take care of it; she would not break her promise, she had said, jamming her chin over the immense plant in her arms. In the end, Evan had lifted her bodily, still gripping the plant, into the saddle. He had tucked the blanket around the plant, as well. Clementine sat on her horse, looking like a big-eyed forlorn orphan in the light, sweeping veil of snow.

He couldn't afford to baby-sit a woman who would most likely destroy everything he had worked to build. The aged mule and the horses couldn't carry all of her boxes and Evan would lose time returning to retrieve them from storage. Evan tucked his chin lower into his collar and turned back to watch the snow- and mud-covered trail and brood over his latest misfortune.

Clementine Barlow—she'd kept her father's name after her divorce—was a disaster, if Evan ever saw one. According to Claudia, Clementine's florist shop was always in a financial bog because of her soft, giving heart—she'd be just great in a profit-making venture, he thought moodily.

Evan inhaled the freezing air and watched mule deer move through the pine trees to a creek. He'd worked too hard to let Jack Barlow's youngest daughter toss away everything. Tough-as-nails Jack Barlow had spawned two of the most vulnerable women Evan had ever met. While Claudia was sensible and quiet, Clementine was energetic and determined to work at his side.

She smelled like some exotic flower, a tang of adventure running through her sweet scent. The cold wind had churned snowflakes and her dainty, elusive fragrance between them, and Evan had found himself inhaling deeply. He was stunned to discover he'd been foraging through the smells of clean soap and laundry softener to Clementine's intimate, feminine scents. Her eyes had looked up at him worriedly when he'd read the note, like big bruised violet petals lying on her milky skin. Her soft lips had trembled as she watched him, reminding him of July's rose petals shimmering with morning dew.

After they'd stored the boxes the mule couldn't carry, Clementine had turned to him. She'd stood on tiptoe, snared his neck and drew him down to kiss his cheek. "Remember...it's for the best. You'll find someone else...."

Angry with his stunned reaction, he'd struck back at her. He'd remembered Claudia's reference to Clementine "left standing at the altar." "Did *you* find someone else?" Evan had demanded ruthlessly.

"Well...I...I wasn't in the market," she had stated unevenly.

He'd felt as though he had stepped on a kitten's tail as her soft bottom lip quivered. She'd touched her flat little hat with her mitten, perhaps for reassurance.

Evan's leather-clad glove tightened on the reins he held so easily. At forty-two, he didn't need hugs and kisses to soothe his wounds. Or a woman whose eyes mourned his scars.

He needed Tanner land under his feet. He still had a few dreams left and one of them was to make the project a success. With the dividends, he intended to create a boys' ranch for needy, troubled teenagers—as he had been.

Clementine Barlow's interference or perhaps her planned takeover or sellout wasn't going to tear apart what he had built.

"Scary," he muttered, thinking about her hugs and kisses and the way he'd allowed himself to be drawn down to receive them. The stallion turned understanding, liquidy brown eyes toward him. Any woman who could hug and kiss and confuse a man that fast needed watching, Evan decided warily, hunching down in his coat against the penetrating winds.

He was more stunned by his instant response—the overpowering need to gather her close and let her hold him tightly. To bury his face in the soft, sweet, yet exotic fragrance.

Evan scowled at snowbirds fluttering over stark, leafless blackberry bushes. Despite Clementine's sympathetic expression, there was a thread of anger riding her. Evan exhaled abruptly. She was probably angry about his reluctance to cry into a flowery, jasmine-scented handkerchief. Clementine was more emotional and volatile than Claudia.

Claudia. He'd wanted to marry her, to lead the safe gentle life a woman like her could give him. He'd cared for her sons and for her. When he'd proposed marriage, she'd nodded and served him another piece of apple pie. He understood that Claudia might have had romantic dreams and that she was settling for "making-do." Evan had promised himself that she would never regret her decision to marry him. He'd been working hard to make a home and an income for them; perhaps he should have taken more time to see her—but Claudia lived a two-hour drive away, after the trail's one-hour horseback ride, and in lieu of visiting her, he'd restructured the Barlow hotel. He'd seen her at Christmas and it was now late March.

Whoever Richard was, he'd claimed Claudia and the boys quickly.

Love. Evan doubted such an emotion existed, but he had intended to give Claudia whatever she needed to be happy. He'd set his mind to learning what pleased her and trying his best to make her feel comfortable with their impending marriage. The boys would be raised on land that had been homesteaded by his family and would have a sense of belonging to an endless chain. That was important, Evan decided as he ducked a snow-laden pine branch—belonging to the land and having children to follow him.

He'd wanted a child with Claudia, but had feared to ask her just yet. She'd trembled when he stood too close, and Evan had been careful not to frighten her.

While he cared for Claudia, if there was anything that he didn't want in his life, it was love. When fate ripped love away, pain and the cost were too dear. The memories of his mother and father arguing bitterly had never healed. After the divorce, his mother had swept him off to Seattle and Evan-the-child had tried his best to survive in a terrifying new world. His mother's death had ripped away another part of his heart, and the return to his embittered, alcoholic father was traumatic. Still, he had loved and cared for Ben Tanner until the end. He was just fifteen when his father died, a year after Evan had lost his thumb in the rodeo.

Evan shifted restlessly in the saddle, the years weighing down on his shoulders. Ben Tanner had lost everything, hating and dying in a shack while his nemesis, Jack Barlow, owned Tanner land.

As that bitter frightened teenage boy long ago, Evan had promised himself he would get the land back into Tanner hands. He was desperately searching for a home when he'd married Angelica. He'd thought he was in love, and the disastrous divorce left him in shreds for years. When he was recovering from a severe back injury, Evan had had hours of thinking time and he realized what would satisfy him. Twenty-four years after Ben Tanner died, Evan had approached Jack Barlow with an offer— to rebuild the old hotel in Bliss and make a profit. With the senior partnership in his hands, Jack had agreed and the Bliss Hotel and Saloon now bore a Barlow name.

In February, Clementine had written stating that she now owned Jack's senior partnership and would be arriving in March. After Clementine experienced the remodeled Barlow hotel and saloon, she'd leave soon enough.

A soft thud and a muffled cry drew his glance over his shoulder. A branch he had ducked had hit Little Miss Do-Gooder in the face. She mopped her mitten across her face, and tenderly dusted snow from her plant, which had peeked out from the blanket. Then she glared at him as if he had caused the incident.

Evan grimly returned his gaze to the trail. He wasn't so happy himself.

Clementine Barlow was not tossing his hard work and plans into the dust. She was not taking over or selling out Tanner land. All he had to do was to wait her out. No sensible woman would stay in a broken-down, barely furnished 1880s hotel-saloon-bawdy house. While vacationing wealthy businessmen enjoyed the challenge of roughing it, the Barlow woman would leave after getting one good look at the barren rooms and bathing facilities—a hot-water kettle and a galvanized tub.

Evan brushed the leather-clad stub of his thumb against his cheek, the side that Clementine had kissed both times. Amid the stubble of his morning beard—he hadn't had

time to shave before beginning the two-hour trek to
Loomis—the brush of her lips remained like the sweeping caress of a rose petal or the wings of an elegant but-
terfly.

Yuma turned to stare at him again as if agreeing with
Evan's mental snort. "Women ... Do-gooders," he muttered and Yuma nodded and nickered.

"What do you mean, 'you can't move'?" Two hours
later, Evan paused in the doorway to the two-story, gray-
board building. He shifted the heavy cardboard box on
his shoulder and waited, glaring at Clementine through
the wash of mist and snow, which had continued through
the journey.

When she shook her head, Evan muttered something
dark and fierce and set the box on the floor inside the hotel's saloon room. He retraced his steps down the wide
front porch to stand beside her horse. "I'm stuck up
here," she admitted between chattering teeth.

Clementine tried to flex her fingers, but the freezing
drizzle and snow had penetrated her mittens. The blanket Evan had tucked over her slid aside, revealing the
bruised leaves of the plant she treasured. The icy wind
lifted a strand of hair along her cheek and swept it to her
throat. One of Jethro's darkening leaves quivered under
her nose and she sneezed. She shivered, a movement that
Evan's sharp gaze noted at once. "Don't tell me. You
didn't wear underwear, right?" he asked flatly.

Her frozen cheeks tingled with a blush that did not appear. Between her chattering teeth, she managed to say,
"My undergarments ... are ... none ... of your business—"

Evan sighed tiredly. "Long johns ... thermal underwear," he explained. "I'm wearing it. You aren't."

"Oh." Evan reached to pluck her into his arms. He carried her into the hotel and kicked the door shut with his heel.

Being swept along by Evan left her little time to study the first floor, but she glimpsed a large, cold, window-filled room.

Clementine clutched the plant tightly as Evan grimly carried her up the stairs and into a large warm room. He placed her on a broken-down sofa covered by a tattered quilt, then stripped away the damp blanket from her. Stunned and unused to being handled like a child, Clementine gripped the plant for emotional support. She watched Evan scowl as he jerked off her boots and socks and began chafing her feet. He knelt in front of her, tucked her feet between his warm thighs and muttered, "Give me that thing," before he took the plant and placed it on the floor.

"Jethro," she murmured, wiggling her toes to see if they were frozen.

"What?" He ripped off her mittens, squeezed her hands once and cursed as he began rubbing them.

"My plant...his name is Jethro. He's lonely for his plant companion, Sissie, who will probably die of frostbite in that store's back room. I'm certain if you would have tried just a bit harder, we could have brought more things.... You are not a patient man, Evan Tanner."

At her eye level, Evan stared at her blankly, then shook his head. He ripped off his coat and placed it over her. The weight settled on her, filled with scents of Evan.

She looked at his big, dark hands chafing her smaller ones and began shivering uncontrollably.

Clementine glanced around the sparsely furnished room and tried not to think about the geography of Evan's body—her feet resting under him, bumping against him intimately as his thighs clamped her calves. His denim-clad bottom was gloriously warm; she tried to stop the reflexive seeking of her toes toward that intimate heat and failed.

Evan's hands paused and he inhaled sharply as he stared at her fingers, which were also flexing.

Tiny dots of perspiration appeared across his upper lip. Clementine glanced away from the whorls of hair at the base of his throat, escaping his thermal underwear and his knit sweater. His perspiration and obvious discomfort were probably due to his heavy clothing.

Because she was nervous, she began talking. "I've been reading the report you sent on your work to restore the old hotel. Though last season was a success with your roughing-it idea, perhaps we should broaden our scope to include women—"

Evan's sharp, angry glance stopped her. "Women?" he asked in a raspy, challenging tone as if his western fences had been breached by rustlers.

"Women are clients—consumers, too.... That equals more profit, Evan. I read the material you sent—it was very thorough. I do have suggestions on marketing... and on the addition of women's programs, like maybe— oh, candle making...and weaving...and herbals..."

Evan stared at her, his frown deepening. "...a girls' ranch later, too," she continued, noting that suddenly the air sizzled between them.

She wiggled her toes and his thighs tightened, the muscles shifting beneath the layers of thermal underwear and denim.

"You're not seeing the advantages of our partnership at the moment, Evan. It's the emotional pain of Claudia's—" She leaned forward just as Evan stopped rubbing her hands and looked directly into her eyes. The moment clung and hovered and stopped, the warmth of his face touching hers, his eyes dark and smoky with messages she didn't understand. She interpreted his expression as shielding pain and moved to kiss his cheek. "Evan, you'll get past this," she said gently.

He turned and their lips brushed and lingered, softly, gently.

He moved his lips slowly across hers, then back again, as if tasting a flower. Clementine's senses swirled as she looked into his eyes.

Evan inhaled sharply, blinked and shook his head as if to clear it. Then he lurched to his feet, and stood glaring down at her as his hands curled slowly into fists. She noted a slight flaring of his nostrils and shivered again.

His gray eyes skimmed her toes, which flexed in response. He stared at them as if they'd committed a major crime.

Evan moved impatiently, stripping away his coat and hers and laying her down on the sofa. He tucked the quilt around her, then strode to the stove and stoked it. "Stay put," he ordered when she began to sit up.

"You don't need to take care of me. I'll be fine in a few minutes," she said unevenly. If she could just stop shivering, she could manage. Clementine glared at him. There he stood, toasty-warm in his thermal underwear, his thick wool navy sweater, his faded denims and his bristling cowboy attitude.

"Sure," he agreed disbelievingly. "Your lips are blue and your teeth are chattering. The neck and cuffs of your sweater are wet and so are your jeans." In two strides he was back to the sofa, sliding it effortlessly to the warmth of the stove. "Don't move."

"Stop demanding and ordering. It won't work with me," she muttered, jerking the quilt up to her chin. "You're transferring your pain to someone else—me. Though I understand, I don't like it."

"Pain?" he asked blankly, then he frowned darkly. "Why didn't you say you were freezing?" he demanded fiercely, looking up at the new boards on the ceiling as if asking for divine intervention. His wintery eyes lasered down to her. "Don't tell me. You're a martyr, boss. That's worse than a complainer. Well, boss, I'll be right back— the animals need tending. Meanwhile, don't move."

She refused to answer, glaring at him as he left the room. "'Boss,'" she repeated darkly, looking around the plain, but comfortable room.

She pushed away the memory of his mouth brushing hers, the sweet lingering warmth as his lips pushed gently into hers. It was an accident, she decided. She'd moved to console him and the slight movement of his head had accidently joined their mouths.

An accident, she repeated to herself as she concentrated on the room in which Evan had been living.

A computer and files occupied two tables arranged in an L shape in one corner. Boxes were neatly stacked beneath the surfaces. When Clementine and Evan had arrived at the hotel, she'd noted the second-story veranda and the glass doors flowing into it from this room.

A double-size wrought-iron bed, neatly made, stood on the opposite end of the room with a small battered dresser. Neatly folded jeans and sweaters were stacked on the dresser. Clementine glanced at the open door to the bathroom, then back to the ornate steel-and-cast-iron blazing stove, which was filling the room with heat. She wallowed in the warmth and found that the worst of her shivers had stopped just as she heard Evan's boots on the stairway.

He opened the door and shouldered into the room, carrying her suitcases. He placed them on the floor and before she could move, he flipped open the latches and began foraging through her clothes. "What...do you think you're doing?" she demanded, struggling beneath the quilt that was tangled around her.

He slammed one suitcase shut and began on the other, then he straightened, turning to her with an expression of disgust. "You don't have anything warm enough in there. Just like I thought—" The next instant, Evan walked to the dresser, jerked out a cream-colored garment with arms and legs and returned. He tossed a ball of heavy work-socks into her lap and waved the underwear in front of her nose. "Thermal underwear. A top and a bottom," he said slowly, distinctly, as if speaking to a child. "Put them on under your clothes. I'm going downstairs to stoke up Big Bertha—the furnace. If you're up to it later, I'll show you around."

She smiled gently. Evan was suffering from heart-break; she could afford to be indulgent.

For a time.

Two

In the downstairs kitchen, Clementine held the cup of hot apple cider that Evan had poured. In the other room, the empty spacious "saloon," Big Bertha—an immense, ornate steel-and-iron furnace—clunked and groaned. A large reclining chair with a blanket and a bed pillow sat beside Bertha.

"This kitchen has potential," she said, noting the large wood cookstove, which had been lighted, and the long table and odd assortment of metal and wood chairs. A big chest-type, deep freezer stood against the wall and Evan jerked open the lid to study the contents. He took out a white package, ripped it open and placed it on the counter.

"Supper...steak," he explained. "The wood stove hasn't been used for cooking. I've been heating bathwater on it, and using it for warmth."

Clementine looked at the large galvanized tub resting in the corner. "Ah, Evan...no hot running water?"

"Not a drop of cold running water, either. The well is deep, but the old pump gave out. We'll need a new one and new pipe running into the place. That's this year's project as soon as the weather warms up." She sensed satisfaction in his reply and he looked at her as he said, "The outhouse is behind the hotel."

"Outhouse? You mean the bathroom upstairs or downstairs isn't functioning?"

"No plumbing yet," he said almost cheerfully. "Don't forget to shut the door on the outhouse. In the summertime, there are always spiders and rattlers—rattlesnakes. But lately there's been a cougar around here who just might want to take up residence."

Her hot apple cider sloshed dangerously close to the cup's rim. "Cougar?"

Evan looked at her steadily. "The spiders aren't a problem just yet. Anytime you want to leave, just let me know."

Clementine placed her cup on the scarred, wooden table. She tapped the rim of the cup with her finger. While Evan needed her help, she would not fall to his obvious need to torment her. She had reasoned that rejection would be his first choice of action. "I'm not going anywhere, Evan. Everything I have is invested in this project."

She noted the new windows and the replaced boards as she walked out into the spacious saloon where Big Bertha was crackling with fire. An assortment of electric carpentry tools were neatly lined on the board flooring. An ornate, weathered door was braced between two wooden sawhorses, and a huge toolbox rested in a corner. A professional-looking blueprint of both floors was tacked to the board walls. An elaborately lettered, weathered sign, Bliss Hotel and Saloon, was propped against another wall.

Clementine smiled, remembering how proud her father had been of backing Evan's idea for a guest ranch and buying the ghost town of Bliss, which was on Tanner land. He'd also delighted in knowing that he owned what had been used as a bawdy or sporting house, where "ladies of the line" had plied their wares to miners.

Clementine thought of the sexual escapades that still echoed from the rip-roaring gold and silver rushes. With very little effort, she could almost hear the heavy breathing, the feminine cries and masculine shouts of sexual fulfillment swirling around her—not that she'd ever heard or issued such primitive sounds.

Lovemaking in her marriage had been clinical and lacking, and Morris had never gotten very serious during their engagement. At the time, she had decided that Morris's strict upbringing was the cause. When she had found him and his secretary rumpling the paper across his desk, Clementine had decided that Morris was only inhibited when making love to herself.

She inhaled slowly, catching Evan's masculine scents. He smelled very clean, very rawly male. She shook herself mentally. "You said you replaced the wooden shingles on the roof and braced up the foundation. You've also replaced the flooring, haven't you? And wired the entire building?"

"Not much else to do around here in the wintertime."

"There's promotion packets and advertising."

Evan jerked on his leather gloves. "Uh-huh. I put one ad in the Seattle newspaper and had more men apply than I could manage."

He tipped back his hat, glanced at her beret and watched her face as he said, "The wood rats are still fighting me for possession. All the windows and doors were gone, and the stairway wasn't worth repairing. I built it from scratch after removing the family of skunks who had lived there for years.''

Clementine thought she heard the sounds of a player piano and women laughing seductively in the shadows. "Were last year's customers happy?"

"Yes. They appreciated being away from women who want to change things," he answered, then walked out the door, leaving her to follow.

The winter winds whipped her beret from her hair. One sweep of Evan's glove caught the navy cloth and crumpled it. "Cute," he said, thrusting it at her.

"You will get over this, Evan. Hearts mend," she said firmly, refusing to be intimidated by his scowl. She placed her beret on her head and held it there with her mitten, daring him to say one more word.

Then she was looking at his broad back as he walked into the small, aged barn. The wind whipped the door away from her grasp and he watched stoically while she battled to close it. He waited, his glove resting on Yuma's mottled rump. "You wouldn't have had anything to do with Claudia's decision, would you?" he asked bluntly as she braced her back against the door.

An old goat ambled across the barn and a rooster with a red comb peered down at her from a rafter. While the goat looked friendly enough, the rooster looked as though he'd like to attack her.

Two mottled greyhounds leaned against Evan's long legs, waiting for the scratching that he finally gave them.

Clementine shifted uneasily within the confines of her maxicoat. Claudia's glowing excitement about Richard's hunger for her had severed Evan's chances for marriage. Clementine had helped Claudia with a battery of magazine quizzes and every one said that Richard suited her better than Evan. Evan did not score well in the sexuality, tingles and romantic moves sections. He had rated especially poor in the quiz on a male counterpart's sensitivity to sexual and romantic invitations. Clementine decided to ignore his question and looked at the mule. "Ah . . . he's rather old, isn't he?"

"Mosey makes it okay." He continued to stare at her, demanding an answer for his question, which she avoided. She wondered if Evan had realized that perhaps he might be sexually impaired.

"Ohh," Clementine murmured sympathetically, moving to stroke the mule's neck. "He's tired. The trip must have been horrible for him."

She glanced around the barn as the greyhounds sniffed her red boots warily. "Is this it, all of it?"

The red rooster hopped down from his rafter to the hay and stalked across the bales, while glaring at her. He seemed more welcoming than the human male. Until he started to stomp at her threateningly.

"His name is Heathcliff." Evan shoved hay into the stalls and poured oats into the troughs. Clementine concluded that he might have sensed he didn't measure up to Claudia's needs and had decided not to press his offer of marriage. He leveled a dark unwelcoming stare at her. "Today isn't the best day to ride over the rest of the six hundred acres."

"Oh. So you and these fifteen men went on an old-fashioned cattle drive complete with a chuck wagon. You branded and roped— Where are the cattle?"

"Down in the meadow where the creek winds through. There's a shed and a stand of trees keeping the wind and snow from them. Ten head of cattle didn't exactly make a herd, so last year I borrowed a few."

"No one was hurt, were they? I mean...someone might have worn red, and bulls like to charge that color, don't they? And branding, that's awfully cruel, isn't it?"

"We didn't have bulls and we dipped the iron in a washable dye, not hot coals."

"Oh. Then bulldogging. Oh, that's right...you said the men had to lasso a post and flip a bag of grain to the earth. You didn't hurt any of the cattle, did you? What if the cows didn't want to go where you wanted them to? What about camping outside and gold panning in the creek? Did the customers really like that? What are the bathroom facilities there?"

Evan paused on his way around Mosey and closed his eyes, then he continued walking straight out of the barn and back to the grand old hotel. He patted his thigh and the greyhounds leapt to follow him. Clementine had little choice but to follow the pets who evidently adored Evan.

The wind howled around the historic hotel, the snow and drizzle lashing at the curtainless windows.

"Gingham would be nice," Clementine said over dinner. She refused the thick steak Evan had cooked and settled for a baked potato and green beans. She wondered if the root cellar in back could be used to grow mushrooms.

"Gingham?"

"Yes, maybe oh ... red-and-white checked with ruffles in the kitchen. When we can, I think we should get some thermal-lined drapes for the saloon. To help save energy. That window would be just perfect for potted herbs in the wintertime. You know, chives ... parsley."

"Uh-huh," he said, the muscles in his jaw tensing just once before he swallowed.

"Plumbing is a necessity, Evan. I think we should make that a top priority," Clementine said, restraining the shudder that moved through her when remembering her visit to the outhouse.

"Uh-huh." He took a deep breath and let it out slowly.

"See? We already agree on the management of the Barlow ranch," she said cheerily. "The adjustment to working with a partner won't be that bad, will it?"

His gaze smoldered and pinned her, and he didn't return her hopeful smile, which died.

Big Bertha creaked and moaned pleasantly downstairs while Clementine pilfered through Evan's computer files on the second floor. Clementine hoped she wouldn't have to go to the outhouse again soon.

Evan sat on the sofa, closed his eyes and mulled his bad luck.

He scratched the greyhound Slide's ears.

When he could find a private moment—Clementine's constant flow of questions left him little thinking room—he would write Claudia a note. He wished the best for her and the boys and he wanted to leave the door open for her to change her mind.

He watched the flame rise in the stove's window and petted Zip, the other greyhound. Yesterday he'd discovered someone had pulled the outhouse over, an old Halloween trick. They'd used a horse and dragged the weathered board building until it lodged between two pine trees. This morning he'd found used motor oil poured over a bale of hay. The mischief cost time and money—commodities that he couldn't afford to spare.

He glanced at Clementine, who was skimming financial reports and jotting notes. Her beret perched almost on the side of her head, the gleaming strands of her hair taking on a rich burnished chestnut color from the lamp.

The small cap represented a monument to their different life-styles. A city woman, Clementine would never fit into rural, make-do western life.

With very little effort, she could ruin the nugget of a bank balance he'd worked so hard to start.

She'd have a fight on her hands if she tried to sell the land, which didn't make sense for a woman like her—silky soft, dream-filled and cheerful. Evan studied her hips on the straight seat of the wooden chair, the shift and flow of the feminine curves beneath the restricting denim.

While Claudia was willowy and soft, Clementine's body was curvy. Claudia's presence was relaxing, but Clementine's was in constant motion, swirling the air around him in feminine scents. The red turtleneck sweater was made tighter by the thermal underwear and when she had gotten cold, two little nubs had appeared— Evan's gaze jerked to her stockinged feet, the underwear escaping her jeans at her ankles. Her toes were wiggling now, just as they had beneath him so intimately earlier.

Evan inhaled sharply. When he'd warmed her hands and feet, he'd been stunned by the sharp, erotic tug of his masculinity, the weight of his arousal pushing against the confines of his jeans. He'd held her soft, pale feminine hands in his calloused ones and knew that her body would be just as tender. Every instinct he possessed told him to lay her down on the sofa, to place his mouth over those provocative little nubs and nibble on them through her red sweater.

He studied his linked hands, resting on his flat stomach.

He rummaged through the memory of his last lovemaking experience, which seemed to have occurred two centuries ago—five years ago, he corrected. That night was a lonely spot; he'd met an old friend and had lingered. They'd made love desperately, quickly, satisfying bodies and leaving an unfulfilled ache an hour later as he slipped out her back door. Since his marriage died, he hadn't nibbled on or tasted a woman for an entire night.

His shocking fierce need to taste began when Clementine's wiggling toes had touched him. Or did it begin when the intriguing tips of her breasts thrust against her sweater?

Somewhere during that intense flash point of sexual desire, he'd had fantasies of carefully cradling Clementine's soft breasts and rounded hips in his hands. He'd wanted to run his fingers through those sleek, shining strands of hair and wallow his face in the feminine, exotic scent.

The bruised amethyst shade of her eyes, filled with tears and sympathy, had stopped him cold. In his lifetime he'd had few people care for his aches.

Evan clamped his lips closed, stopping a low hungry groan that came from the depths of his soul. The greyhounds looked up at him sympathetically.

He was off-balance now, affected by Claudia's note. He'd genuinely liked Claudia and her rejection had stung, not an emotion that he allowed himself. Maybe the nuances of the past were creeping around the shadowy corners of the hotel, the sensuality of bygone love affairs seeping into him. A woman like Clementine was made for love, marriage to the right man and a houseful of babies, and after his parents' and his own divorce, he wouldn't let his heart indulge in that tender emotion.

He glanced at her hips shifting on the hard wooden surface of the chair and cursed silently as his body hardened uncomfortably. Because he was aching, emotionally and physically, he stood abruptly and ran his hands through his hair. The movement helped to dislodge the thought of cupping that soft bottom in his palms.

The old bed that he had retrieved and restored from the clutter in the hotel beckoned to him. He could almost hear the springs creaking, the sexual cries of pleasure curling around the firelit, warm room.

Clementine turned, tilted her head as she listened and looked up at him questioningly. "Was that Big Bertha?" she asked.

"Yes," Evan answered flatly, then instinctively lashed out at the source of his discomfort. "You'll have a fight on your hands if you decide to sell out Jack's senior partnership."

Clementine's mobile mouth tightened. Evan noted the usually soft line had an intriguing dip on her upper lip. "I can't buy you out, and I'm not selling out to you," he added, locking his legs at the knee.

She smiled serenely. "Likewise.... My portion of the partnership isn't for sale, either. I don't have money to buy you out, anyway, Evan. I've explained in my letter and when we met in Loomis that I intend to be your partner."

Clementine took a deep breath and lifted her head. "I've come—not only because I've invested my entire life savings in this venture, but because I, too, want to end the Barlow and Tanner unhappy past. I found the feud's whole story in my father's old trunk.... I want to ease the damage my grandmother Elise created when she ran off to marry Roy Barlow instead of marrying Jed Tanner— your grandfather—as she had promised. It is time the Barlows made amends for the bad luck that began when she jilted Roy. Now Claudia has decided—well, she answered questionnaires to make up her mind and Richard's high sensuality decided the matter—" Clementine clamped her lips closed over the last remark.

She straightened her shoulders.

She stood slowly and walked back and forth on the braided rug in front of the stove, locked in her thoughts. Whiffs of feminine scents swirled around Evan who resented his sensual awakening after years of abstinence. He ran his trembling hand through his hair and found Clementine's dark blue eyes watching him.

"Evan, this isn't the end of the world," she said gently.

"What?"

She rested one hand on his forearm and looked up at him, her expression that of concern. "Think about it like this," she offered softly, rubbing his arm soothingly. "You and Claudia were just not romantically suited."

His black eyebrows lifted. "Romantically?" he asked warily.

"You don't fit the profile. Claudia and you would have never been totally happy." Her hand patted his arm before moving away.

"Profile?" he repeated and wondered when he could jump on her thought-train to nowhere.

"Questionnaires. Quizzes. Profiles of lovers. Seeing how well-suited one lover is for another." Her hand slashed out into the air, stirring her feminine scents between them. She began to walk back and forth on the rug and Evan found himself staring at those two little sweater-covered nubs. Clementine leveled him a thoughtful gaze. "Let's dissect your reasons for wanting to marry Claudia. Then perhaps you'll understand better why she decided to end the relationship and marry Richard...whom she loves in a very deep and sexual way."

Clementine's last words were spoken very carefully, emphasizing a point that went whizzing by Evan's grasp. "Go right ahead. I'm listening," he invited gingerly.

She ticked off the reasons on the fingers of one hand. "To provide a safe home for Claudia and her boys. To unite the Tanner and Barlow families and end a century-long feud. You would provide Claudia with nearly all of her needs—" Clementine studied her third finger, which was about to be raised, and lowered it.

She took a deep breath, which raised her breasts, and something dark and sweet and raw started surging in Evan. He was stunned to discover that his jeans were suddenly uncomfortably tight. He sat carefully.

Clementine stopped walking back and forth and placed her hands on her waist, tightening the sweater across her chest. She looked incredibly soft. Evan swallowed deeply. "You see, Evan..."

She cleared her throat and wrung her hands before kneeling between his knees, her hands resting lightly on his thighs. "Oh, Evan..."

Her breasts rested on the sofa seat between his legs. Her eyes begged him to understand. Evan was understanding the full alert of his body, the need to bear Clementine down to the rug and spread himself over her curved, agile, restless body. To warm himself and to nestle in the sweet promise of her softness—

"Sex isn't everything, Evan," she continued softly, looking up at him, tears shimmering in her eyes. One drop caught the light, glistening on her lashes.

A fierce desire to bend and kiss away that teardrop hummed through Evan's body. He swallowed slowly, realizing that he also wanted to kiss every inch of Clementine's pale, curvy body.

"Oh, Evan. How awful to be injured—to lose your thumb in the rodeo and then your—" Clementine's blush rose from her throat.

Evan wondered how she would look lying beneath him, flushed from lovemaking.

Her fingers slipped over his hands, which were digging into his thighs. Clementine's scents wafted around him and he knew that if ever anything would soothe his pain, the cold and the scars that seemed lodged in his life, making love—now, here with this woman—would.

Looking up into his eyes, Clementine placed her hands on his shoulders. "Evan...I have come to rescue you," she whispered gently.

He stared at her for a long moment, reluctant to leave the soft, warm images of Clementine cuddling him on the old wrought-iron bed, of him making long, thorough love to her— "What?" he asked cautiously.

The lamplight gleamed on her hair as she tilted her head and a strand slid across her pale cheek. "I have some experience in psychology and analyzing personal traumas. I've read magazine articles and I'm learning to interpret dreams. We can tell a lot about our basic problems by paying attention to our dreams, you know. Let me help you, Evan. You can learn to lead a full, happy life—"

"What are you talking about?" he asked slowly.

"I'm going to help you through the pain of losing Claudia until you recover emotionally and then we'll work on your recognition of..." She cleared her throat. "Other problems."

Evan placed his hand on Clementine's beret, pushed slightly and when she eased away, he swung one leg over her head and stood up. She remained on the braided rug, her legs curled beneath her, and her arm resting on the sofa. Evan took two strides, then realized that he was not going to pace as she had done earlier. "Lady, if there is anything—anyone—I don't need now, it's a little miss do-gooder."

Clementine smiled in her understanding, irritating way. "I believe you may have an inbred and perhaps justified need for revenge against the Barlow family that your conscious mind does not recognize. Bitterness is not good for the soul. Now that Claudia has—well, jilted you, you could be damaged beyond your physical problems. It is my obligation to rescue you from more pain at Barlow hands."

Evan thrust his hands deep into his back pockets. "Lady, *you* are a pain," he stated flatly.

Her eyebrows shot up, then she smiled again in that maternal, understanding way. "I expected you to react this way, Evan. Defense is probably what you know best. But I'm here now, and I'm fully prepared to take care of you. To walk you through your traumas and encourage you to lead a full, rich life, despite your past experiences."

"Uh-huh." He stared at her warily, then ran his fingers through his hair. He took a deep breath, reached for Clementine's upper arms and lifted her to sit on the sofa. She curled her legs beneath her and waited.

"You're here to rescue me," he repeated slowly and wondered when anyone had ever lent him a helping hand.

She nodded firmly. "And to make your dreams come true. I understand your need to begin a boys' ranch when it is financially possible—though I think a girls' ranch is a definite must."

Evan allowed his gaze to slowly trail down, then back up her curved, soft body, lingering on her breasts, which he fiercely wanted to taste and hold and caress. Her toes wiggled restlessly and her fingers locked together as she smiled in that sweet, placid I-know-I-know way. "You're hurting . . . suffering from Claudia's selection of Richard. But it is for the best. You didn't suit her—fit the profile that she felt was compatible with her needs. Rejection is always hard to take, especially when—" She cleared her throat again. "Especially when a man has . . . certain problems."

"I am managing my problems just fine, Clementine," Evan explained tightly.

She caught his hand, holding it between hers and drawing it to her chest. "Recognition of one's problems is a first step in the right direction. You'll see."

"I don't need rescuing," Evan stated flatly, sensing he was falling into her soft, blue eyes. "Especially by you."

He carefully extracted his hand from the location of her chest. His knuckles had just barely touched the swell of her breasts. "I am doing just fine, Clementine . . . just fine. I would appreciate it very much if you would get out of my problems. From what I understand, you have had a few of your own."

Clementine shifted uncomfortably, her eyes looked away from his, then she touched the beret with her fingers. "Well . . . yes."

Evan smiled. "Then you might want to resolve them and stay out of mine."

Clementine's dark blue eyes locked with his. "I am staying, Evan."

"There is one bed, lady. People will talk about how it is being used." Evan's body hardened instantly as he thought about the old bed's history, and the way Clementine would look snuggled beneath the worn quilt, her face rosy with sleep and desire, her hair spread across the pillowcases. He took his logic one step further. "We'll be alone until Cookie arrives next month—she's an old sourdough, a woman prospector, who helps me in the summer. She's holed up in her cabin for the winter."

Looking up at him, Clementine touched his thigh and every cord in Evan's body went on red-hot alert. "I am unafraid of gossip. We're both past our heated youth and you have a problem— "

She looked at him warily as though changing mental directions. "I can sleep on the floor. Or downstairs on the chair next to Big Bertha. But I'm not worried about being alone with you, Evan."

He moved away from her, restless with the desire humming through his body. "Maybe I don't want you to rescue me, Clemmie. Just maybe I want you to take your pity and that snappy little hat you're wearing on back to Seattle."

Her eyes rounded and she stood slowly. Without her red boots, she barely reached his shoulder, yet she looked up at him fearlessly. "Evan, no one has called me 'Clemmie' since Claudia and I were young girls. I prefer Clementine," she said very precisely. Then she paused and smiled tightly. "You're tired. You'll feel better in the morning."

"Uh-huh. When you pack it on out of here."

Clementine studied him as he loomed over her. "You know, Evan, Claudia never said anything about you acting passionate about anything. I distinctly remember that she said you never showed your emotions."

Her fingers smoothed away a strand of hair that was crossing his forehead and his scowl. Evan jerked away from her touch and Clementine pressed her hand over his. She looked at him worriedly. "Right now, you seem to be on some sort of emotional edge."

Evan backed away from her and found his back to the wall. Clementine looked up at him with her big dark blue eyes, and whispered softly, "Oh, Evan. You need a hug..." Then she wrapped her arms around his waist and hugged him briefly.

When she moved away, Evan leaned against the wall for support and tried to steady his breathing. He'd been taken by surprise again, unable to move as Clementine's scents swirled around him, tangling his senses.

He blinked, watching Clementine walk slowly away, the gentle sway of her hips causing him to sweat.

The impression of her breasts, the ones he'd wanted to nibble and taste, remained in his midsection. Evan ran the flat of his hand across his stomach and found it aching. A hot tremor of desire ricocheted through his taut body. "Clementine," he said rawly, uncomfortably, "You... are...a...loose cannon. You can't just grab me and hug me at will."

The firelight splashed a warm rich red glow over her hair as she pivoted and looked at him sadly. "Evan. Trust me. If ever a man needed hugs and kisses, it is you. Think of me as the sister you never had."

Three

Evan placed the hammer back in his toolbox, then stripped off his gloves and looked around the looming shadows of the first-floor saloon. At eleven o'clock in the evening of Clementine's first day on the Barlow Guest Ranch, Evan was cold to the bone and disgusted with the assortment of aches that had returned from his rodeo and construction days. After spending the last four hours checking on the cattle and repairing the barn wall that Mosey had ventilated with his back hooves and mulling over the reaction he'd had to Clementine's body, Evan wanted mind-blanking sleep.

He wanted to forget about red-checkered gingham curtains that matched the kitchen tablecloth, about potted chives growing on the windowsill, about adding weaving and candle making to the ranch's program, and having a hoard of troubled girls invade the business he had created and nurtured into one successful year.

He ripped off his hat, sailed it to a waiting wall hook and jerked off his coat. The greyhounds padded after him as he walked through the shadows of the main saloon room, following the light and the delicious scents coming from the kitchen. He lifted the note on the table. It read:

Have one. I think we could make these on the chuck-wagon cookout with very little problem. Don't worry about me. You take the bed. I'm sleeping on the floor. I tried the sofa. It has lumps. We need a new one and new kitchen tea towels.

Clementine

His eyes ran across the last sentence. "That's just fine, boss. You find some extra money," he muttered grimly before crushing the note and tossing it into the bin he used for the stove's kindling. A new sofa wasn't on his list of necessary purchases. He lifted the tattered kitchen towel covering the pans on the kitchen table and discovered freshly baked apple dumplings—pastry-covered apples in a sweet, buttery syrup. Evan dipped one steaming dumpling into a bowl, spooned syrup over it and fought enjoying every delicious bite while he debated the issue of the woman sleeping on the cold floor upstairs. He couldn't leave her there; she'd be stiff and sick by morning.

Evan shook his head and dipped another juicy dumpling into his empty bowl. He'd sleep on the chair beside Big Bertha, and Clementine would eventually discover that the bed was warmer than the floor.

Minutes later, Big Bertha crackled with fire and Evan lay in the old chair, clad in his boxer shorts. He listened for creaking sounds from the bed upstairs, tugged the blanket across his bare legs and waited.

A half hour later, he crouched by Clementine Barlow, studying the woman who had invaded his life. He placed his hand on his side, rubbing the ache lodged in ribs that he had broken long ago.

Clementine reminded him of the ten-year-old girl who'd run across his path just as he was riding in and winning an endurance race. He'd broken two ribs when he reined his horse to one side, saving the girl.

In his worn sleeping bag, one hand flung beside her head, the reddish tints in her brown hair catching the light, Clementine did not look like a woman determined to take away Tanner land; in fact, she did not look like a thirty-six-year-old woman.

Yet she'd been married—according to Claudia—at twenty-two and divorced at twenty-six.

Evan ran the stub of his thumb across his cheek as he often did when his thoughts ran deep. Above the neckline of thermal underwear, a vein slowly beat in Clementine's throat. She moved, and cinnamony scents mixed with jasmine and a feminine fragrance jarred Evan's dark thoughts.

The greyhounds' noses lifted instantly, sniffing, reminding him of his unique reaction when Clementine was near, and the thought nettled. Evan pointed a finger at the door, and with their tails between their legs, the dogs padded out of the room.

Moving quickly, he tugged the sleeping bag's zipper down and slid his arms beneath Clementine's pliable body. When he lifted her, she sighed and wrapped her arms around his neck, snuggling closely to him, her cold face buried in the warm curve of his throat and shoulder.

Evan tensed. He stood still, braced his legs against the added weight and tried to force himself to move, carrying her to the bed. He had just turned back the sheets and intended to slide Clementine between them.

She sighed and nuzzled his throat with her cold nose.

Her breasts flowed, unbound against his chest.

Evan forced himself to breathe slowly, though his heart was racing against the feminine softness of her breasts. A tiny feminine nub etched a maddening pattern against his chest each time she breathed.

He swallowed, realizing that his throat was suddenly very dry. Walking stiffly, trying to push away the delicate, warm brush of her breath against his skin, Evan managed to carry Clementine to the bed. He lowered her gently, only to have her arms tighten. "I'm cold," she murmured, hugging him fiercely and scooting over on the bed to give him room.

When Evan tried to draw away, Clementine's grip tightened and on the verge of falling into bed, Evan sat carefully. He tried to draw away.

"No," she murmured sleepily, moving against him, and Evan found himself lying beside her. He began to move away and her arms tightened.

Each time he tried to extract himself from her arms, she snared him closer, cuddling and snuggling to him for warmth. She nuzzled his chest, foraging through the hair there to the hard warmth of his skin. She turned, wrapped an arm and a leg around him, sighed deeply and found his toes with hers.

Her cold slender feet nestled against his, wiggling restlessly until he clamped his larger feet around them, an instinctive, protective movement.

Her toes wiggled once, then stilled. Evan swallowed, breathing lightly as the flames in the stove crackled and the scent of cinnamon and jasmine and woman swirled around him. He lay ramrod straight, aware that the old bed had shifted Clementine's weight against him.

In his lifetime, he'd moved exactly as he wanted, when he wanted. The experience of being tethered by silky hair, exotic and feminine fragrances, and slender, soft limbs stunned him. He moved his hand uneasily from her shoulder to her back and she arched against his touch like a cat under a petting.

"Mmm... Buddy-Bear...my Buddy-Bear. Clemmie loves Buddy-Bear," Clementine crooned in a whisper.

Evan blinked as she burrowed closer. He replaced his hand to her shoulder, his fingers settling over the curve of it and denying his move away from her. Then a flip of her hand drew the blankets over them. "Go to sleep, Buddy-Bear. I'll keep you safe," she whispered sleepily and curled against him, snaring him with one arm and one leg.

Evan had never been cuddled in his life. The thought that in her sleep Clementine considered him huggable and cuddly as a stuffed toy, astonished him.

He remembered again suddenly that he had never stayed an entire night in a woman's bed since his youthful marriage twenty-three years ago.

Silky soft, fragrant strands slid across his cheek to his mouth. Another strand curled around his ear and one rode his throat like a silken necklace. Evan found his fingers locked around Clementine's wrist, her pulse beating slowly beneath his touch.

He inhaled sharply and knew he had to get out of that bed.

All he had to do was to unsnare himself and slide away.

He blew a silky tendril from his nose.

He couldn't move away any more than he could stop breathing.

Evan allowed the warmth and the woman's softness and scents to envelop him, soothing the aching cold shadows that had clung to him for a lifetime.

Evan decided to linger in this bed with this woman just long enough to get warm—or at least before she awoke.

He nuzzled the top of her head. While she was sleeping, Clementine Barlow didn't seem a problem. He'd leave in a few minutes....

Clementine tugged Buddy-Bear closer to her, enjoying his fuzzy warmth beneath her cheek. She always slept better, snuggled next to the giant bear her father had won for her at a carnival. She hugged him tighter and eased her leg over him. Buddy-Bear grumbled in a deep raspy tone and turned to her.

Clementine awoke to the sound of gently creaking springs and Evan's big hand sliding under her thermal shirt to find and caress her breast. He murmured something in her hair, his index finger prowling over the tip of her softness, circling the hardening nub.

His next murmur held a low pleased intimate, growling sound that raised Clementine's eyebrows.

Resting intimately between her legs, Evan's masculinity did not reflect the sexual affliction that the sisters had decided plagued him.

Clementine held very still.

She swallowed gently as Evan's large palm sought her other breast and began caressing it gently, slowly, luxuriously.

Heat ran through him like an electrical charge, humming from his large hard body to hers. Clementine blinked, then carefully placed her two hands on his wrist to draw his hand from her breast.

Evan grumbled something and for an instant his hand closed over her possessively, as if nothing could take her away from him. Then he allowed her to draw his hand away and she eased from the bed.

Forty-five minutes later, Clementine looked at the dawn breaking outside the kitchen window. She waved a kitchen towel over the smoke rising from the old cookstove. She'd stoked kindling into it, anxious to cook breakfast on it her first morning as Evan's working partner.

Clementine jerked the skillet of burning bacon from the wood stove to the electric stove's burner—next to the coffeepot, which had boiled over. She continued to flap the towel at the smoke and think about awakening to find Evan's hard-muscled body tangled with hers, his breath blowing the rumpled strands of hair on top of her head.

She caught the odor of burning toast and reached to jerk the cord on the toaster, which was developing a smoke cloud of its own.

Evan had moved her into the bed to be kind.

Since her dreams had revolved around holding her old Buddy-Bear, she'd probably latched on to Evan thinking he was her long-ago, immense cuddly toy.

Evan's chest was furry, the texture delighting her fingers just as Buddy-Bear had. Of course, Evan's chest was hard and had two masculine nubs.

Clementine remembered the sight of Evan sprawled on the old bed, his blue black hair tousled across the white pillowcase, his jaw covered with dark stubble that ran down into a broad, darkly tanned chest. After she had dressed quickly in her sweater and jeans, she had stood over him, daring to draw the cover that had sagged low on his stomach up to his chest. Her fingers had ached to smooth that crisp, gleaming wedge of black hair covering his chest and she'd pushed them into her back pocket. She wouldn't attack Evan in his sleep, abusing his lacking sexuality. She swallowed, almost choking on the smoke layering the room.

Through the gray haze, she caught a movement at the doorway and Evan stalked through the smoke. He glared at her, then flipped a silver mechanism on the stove's pipe. He spoke slowly, distinctly as the smoke stopped churning from the old stove. "This is a damper. Has to be opened when you stoke up the fire. Smoke goes up through the pipe. I partially close it at night to keep the fire burning slowly."

"Oh." Clementine tried not to stare at the broad width of his bare chest and the intriguing vee of dark hair down to the unsnapped waistband of his jeans.

He stared down at her as though he wanted to say more, then pivoted and jerked open a window, allowing fresh, freezing air into the kitchen. He flapped the T-shirt he had been carrying in one hand, then crossed his arms over his bare chest and continued staring at her while she poured coffee into cups and placed them on the table. "You," he said ominously, glancing at the beret on her head, "are not a country girl."

Clementine drained the bacon carefully, placing it on plates with the burned toast. Actually, she was a good cook, but the stove had bewildered her. It was a challenge, and she liked rising to challenges very much. She refused to be intimidated by Evan's ill temper on her first morning at the Barlow Guest Ranch. "Shall we eat? You'll feel better with a good breakfast in you."

Evan closed the window. He looked at the filled plates and cups on the table. "Let's get this straight, Clementine...I am not a breakfast person," he said warily, though he walked to the table. He jerked on the T-shirt and sat as if preparing to face a firing squad or an argument.

Clementine sat opposite him and something inside her mourned the magnificent muscled chest that he had just covered. If ever a man's chest was designed for a woman to rest her head upon, it was Evan's.

Evan took one look at her, then considered his breakfast, which he ate stoically. She picked at hers, then dipped an apple dumpling into a bowl and stood to place it in the heating shelf of the old wood stove. She returned to her place. "My father was always in a bad mood in the mornings, too. Claudia and I are morning people and always quite cheerful then, though we seem to drift off a bit early in the evenings."

Evan grimly chewed the toast she had just buttered and replaced in his plate. She wondered if the subject of the shared bed would plop on the breakfast table or if she should serve it up to him. She fiddled with her fork, then jumped up to retrieve the warmed dumplings. She took away the plate with the burned food and put the apple dessert in its place. Evan glared at her. "There," she said cheerily, unwilling to have her morning ruined by the secret stove-damper thing or a sulking cowboy. "No need to eat a burned breakfast."

He inhaled slowly, stretching the old T-shirt across his chest. "Thanks. These are good."

"Think nothing of it." She was making real progress with Evan. He was savoring the apple dumpling, his bearded jaw moving rhythmically.

Evan sipped the coffee warily and tried to concentrate on the crossword puzzle he had been working on before she'd arrived. He'd ripped the puzzle from a magazine and had spent hours working on it at the table. Now it offered a distraction from the woman who had invaded his life. He picked up the pencil and tapped it on the one word that had evaded him, despite a search through the dictionary.

"Bouquet," Clementine offered.

He glanced at her and she smiled gently. "Bouquet fits the last down space."

"Uh-huh. I know," Evan lied and scratched in *bouquet,* then tossed down his pencil in disgust. Clementine had ripped away the taunting challenge of the crossword puzzle.

"I'm used to an electric pot," she was explaining as he dealt with his irritation over the crossword puzzle. "I didn't see any juice in the freezer. You should have juice and whole-grain cereal every morning. I couldn't find the cereal, either."

Evan inhaled slowly and deeply again. He leveled a dark, smoldering look at her, but said nothing, which seemed encouraging to Clementine. She decided to press her thoughts while he was enjoying the apple dumpling. She tapped the notes she had brought down from the office-living space. "I don't notice deductions for insurance premiums. We'll have to have insurance—a company policy for employees."

"Fine," he said without enthusiasm and finished the dessert. He leaned back in his chair, smoothing the old chipped coffee cup with his hands. Clementine watched his dark fingers moving on the heavy white porcelain and thought of the calluses she had discovered against her breast earlier. His hand tightened on the warm cup as he noticed the wispy bra and rosebud-patterned panties she had washed and hung near the stove to dry.

Clementine sat very straight. "I think we should research insurance that would offer therapy for problems such as yours. I'll start making calls right away."

One dark eyebrow shot up. "My problems?"

She shifted uneasily on the chair. Though Evan hadn't moved, she sensed his masculine antennae were twitching, catching any nuances and filtering them into his thoughts. Despite his relaxed pose, he was very alert, like a panther she'd seen once in a zoo, lounging on a sunny branch. His tail had twitched lazily while he watched his female counterpart walk by him.

Clementine swallowed. She wasn't anyone's female counterpart and she frankly doubted that she ever had been. Her ex-husband, James, and Morris, her ex-fiancé, had not seemed overly stimulated. In fact, James had once stopped his clinical lovemaking when he remembered where he had placed a valued stamp for safekeeping.

Something tight and hot clenched deep within her as she remembered the luxurious way Evan's fingers had caressed her breast. She hoped he would not notice the flush strolling up her throat to her cheeks. She doubted that he would be distracted by a stamp once he set his mind to having what he wanted. In something other than lovemaking, of course.

"Look," he said impatiently. "Nothing happened last night. You were cold on the floor... and I lifted you into bed. I was too tired to get up again, that's all. Nothing happened," he repeated darkly.

"Oh, I know," she soothed. "Of course nothing could happen. I wasn't worried."

The smoke-scented air shifted between them as Evan studied her carefully. "'Nothing could happen'?"

She leaned forward, eager to explain her thoughts on the new insurance policy, which the conversation had just opened. She looked into Evan's dark gray eyes and decided she needed to be on her feet, where she did her best thinking. She rose and began pacing back and forth across the kitchen. "Well...it's obvious, Evan. The therapy—or perhaps hospitalization—that you might require is very expensive. Since we know there is a problem—"

She stopped pacing and tried to soften the blow with a kind smile before continuing. "We can get a policy to allow for therapy for your...ah...sexual dysfunction problem...ah...your injury."

Evan stood slowly, and suddenly the spacious kitchen seemed very small as Clementine took a step backward. She cleared her throat, refusing to be intimidated when he walked slowly to her.

"Tell me more about my 'sexual dysfunction,'" he invited in a low raspy tone that reminded her of a wolf growling a warning to his prey.

Clementine looked up, her back colliding softly with the wall. "Evan, Claudia and I worked for days to collect enough profiles—questionnaires—to determine your level of sexuality."

"Go on," he murmured, placing both hands on the wall beside her head and looking down at her.

"Nothing could have happened last night, Evan. We both know it," she whispered as gently as she could. "But with therapy, you could probably be intimate—stimulated by the woman you love— You see, Claudia just needed...more. She needed...uh..."

Evan's hard mouth curved and Clementine hoped she was making progress with the delicate matter of his damaged sexuality. He toyed with a strand of her hair and studied it thoughtfully.

"You know, Clemmie, the first thing in the morning might not be the time to talk to a man about therapy for his sexuality...his *dysfunctioning* sexuality. Especially since he's spent the night being called 'Buddy-Bear' and getting squeezed and hugged.''

Evan's dark gaze rested on her lips, which had just dropped open, and Clementine sucked in her breath.

Then very carefully, Evan drew her from the wall and took her in his arms.

She blinked, aware of the hardness of Evan's thighs braced against her softer ones. His big, warm hand slid up to knead the tense muscles at the nape of her neck. Evan lowered his mouth and fitted it perfectly over the shape of hers.

The sweet touch stunned her, her last thought of Evan's dysfunctioning sexuality swirling away in the remnants of the smoky scents. Her fingers locked to his shoulders for support as he drew her very close—so close, his heart thudded heavily into her body, as if he were claiming her, making her a part of him.

His lips kissed and tantalized, nibbling her bottom lip and playing in the soft corners of her mouth until Clementine raised both arms and locked them around the strength of his shoulders.

Evan's big hands stroked and molded, smoothed and caressed a path down to her hips. His fingers spread open beneath her bottom and he lifted gently until Clementine's legs were locked around his hips.

The dizzying kiss went on. Evan made a raw hungry noise deep in his throat and his tongue flicked gently at her lips as he gathered her closer. She tightened her arms and legs around him and Evan inhaled sharply, the warmth of his face burning against hers. He breathed unevenly. Or was it her?

She realized distantly that her fingers were digging into the muscles of his back. She realized that Evan trembled within the lock of her arms and legs and that he was very, very warm and very intense as he gently moved his lips away from hers.

The gentle nibbling kisses softened and eased and Evan's smoke-colored eyes were watching her. His thumbs caressed her hips lazily. "Clemmie," he whispered huskily as she flushed and forced her fingers to unlock from his shoulders.

"Goodness," she whispered back, staring at him and licking her sensitive lips. She tingled and melted from head to toe, aching little prickles lodged deep within her femininity, and a series of old-fashioned quivers ran through her.

She blinked and Evan kissed the tip of her nose...then each set of eyelashes. "Well, Clemmie? Do you still think that nothing could have happened?"

She cleared her throat, too aware of his hard thrusting body against hers. "I understand that you are experimenting," she murmured very carefully.

His black eyebrows shot up. "What?"

She smoothed the tense muscles beneath his T-shirt with her fingertips. A quiver ran beneath her touch and Clementine lifted her hand. "You've just realized that there is a possible problem and you were testing the depth of your new knowledge with me. It's what I would want to do."

"Huh," he answered flatly. "What do you know about that." There was no question in his statement and she sensed anger just beneath the surface of his bland expression. "You can let me go now," he offered, as his hands slowly lowered her until she stood in front of him.

Clementine pushed away the need to lock her legs around him again. Evan loomed over her, his hand trembling as he soothed away a swathe of hair from her hot cheek. He touched her gently, exquisitely, running his fingertips across the flush covering her cheeks and across her tender lips. She stood very still under his touch and when she opened her eyes, Evan's hard mouth had softened, his eyes warm with humor. "So if you suddenly realized you had a...sexual problem...you would want to experiment? Do you have a problem, Clemmie?"

"Me? Of course not."

Evan's gray eyes smoldered, then slowly looked down at her breasts. Clementine followed his gaze and flushed when she saw the hard nubs just barely touching him. "You are one soft woman," Evan stated huskily, distinctly, as he continued to stare at her breasts.

When she realized it had been several heartbeats since she'd breathed last, Clementine breathed deeply, unsteadily, and her breasts rose to touch his chest. Evan's gaze jerked to hers, shocking her with his hunger. She leaned back, struck by the force of his need. Of course Evan was just experimenting, she reminded herself. He was just off-balance with his new knowledge and uncertain about himself. She could offer him the kindness of a few experimental kisses, she decided.

"Watch out, little do-gooder," he warned softly, tugging a strand of her hair, and then he was gone.

Clementine walked unsteadily to a chair and plopped into it. While Evan was experimenting, realizing that he did have a sexual problem, she had her own problems.

Like the aching need to bear Evan to the kitchen floor and vamp him. She watched a bird walking back and forth on the windowsill. It wouldn't be right for her to take advantage of Evan and explore her own steaming sensuality.

She gripped the tea towel and twisted it in her hands, fighting the unusual need to strangle Evan for leaving her. She forced her fingers to release the towel. Her mood was unreasonable, of course. The restless surging of emotion was due to simple surprise when Evan had acted so quickly.

Not that any man had acted hungrily or quickly when near her. She allowed herself one tremble and just one curling of her toes in her red boots. She flexed her fingers and straightened her beret. Her need to arch into his arms and tighten her legs around—goodness, she had actually leg-locked Evan! Clementine inhaled sharply, remembering the hardness of his body.

Evan was testing his problem when he'd lifted her bottom in his big hands.

Clementine placed her fingertips at the base of her throat and discovered her pulse was racing.

She moistened her sensitized lips and remembered the gentle, seeking flick of his tongue. Clementine trembled. Just for an instant, she had thought of taking him inside, deepening the kiss. Just for a moment, she'd wanted to take—aggressively assert her needs . . . like jerking up his T-shirt and pressing herself against that broad, beautiful, masculine chest.

Until this moment in her lifetime, she hadn't felt really, truly greedy about anything. But just at that moment, when Evan had been discovering and testing his problem, she did want to experiment a bit herself.

She did not feel passive as she had with her ex-husband and with Morris's tentative kisses. She'd felt fiery-hot and hungry.

Her beret began sliding from her head and she realized she'd been trembling. She firmly replaced the symbol of her new, daring life.

Her fingers pressed against her throat. She had to protect Evan now and it was wrong of her to take advantage of him. It was also important that Evan realize he was not nudging her away from the Barlow Guest Ranch by ill temper or devastating kisses.

Four

———

"**So** you rescued the greyhounds when they couldn't race? When they became frightened of the starting bell and their owner was going to dispose of them?" Clementine asked early that afternoon. She slid from her horse and came to stand beside the sleigh, which Evan had used to haul hay to the cattle.

"Uh-huh." Evan gripped the bale of hay and grimly carried it to a feeder. After learning that Claudia thought him sexually impaired and his reaction to Clementine's sweet kiss and trembling body had squashed the theory, Evan was painfully uncomfortable. He realized that if Clementine had parted her lips and the kiss had deepened, nothing could have kept him from spreading her out on the table and sampling her like her mouth-watering apple dumplings.

Clementine Barlow's response had thoroughly unnerved him. Though it had been years since he'd felt the taut, unyielding potency of desire, he knew that if ever he wanted a woman, he wanted Clementine. The sweetness and trust beneath her kiss beguiled and intrigued him. He'd wanted to nuzzle and cuddle and roll with and—Evan tossed the bale into the feeder just as he wanted to toss away any emotions that came near wanting, or needing, or love.

Another woman might have been frightened or might have deepened the sensuality running like lightning between them. But Clementine had just held him tightly in the soft snare of her arms and legs as though he were Buddy-Bear.

He cut the twine and circled his hand with it, stuffing it into his pocket and watching the cattle come to feed. He was about to dump grain pellets into a trough when he realized Clementine was gripping the back of his jacket for support on the slippery snow and standing beside him. He stood very still, unused to the gentle tether. Then he turned slightly, keeping the wind from her as she scanned the cattle and the countryside. Fresh, feminine scents sailed up at him and caused him to catch his breath. "Oh, how lovely, Evan. I see why you love it so," she whispered.

He realized that he was frightened, afraid to look down at her. Afraid he'd drag her to him again. "Yes," he said simply.

"To know that years ago, our ancestors stood just like this... absorbing the fierce, wild beauty—"

"'Our'? As in both of our ancestors together? Your grandmother did not marry my grandfather," Evan noted firmly. "The bride said no."

Clementine looked up at him, her mitten holding back a shining skein of hair. "You'll get over Claudia, Evan.

Time heals wounds of the heart.'' She looked away and added softly, ''And it heals other things, as well.''

''I thought we settled that sexually impaired business, Clemmie,'' Evan stated in a low, ominous tone. She smiled at him in a kind, soothing, motherly way and he wanted to jerk her to him and taste those rosy-red lips again. Instead, he moved warily away. He wasn't in the mood for one of her stunning fast hugs and sisterly kisses.

Clementine Barlow was a woman who gathered loving relationships like a flower gathered bees. Evan tensed, very aware of Clementine's nearness; if there was one thing he didn't want, it was a relationship based on love. With Claudia, he understood the mutual basis of friendship and of filling needs. That is, he thought the relationship was working without the element of love until Clementine's magazine profile of a lover had sent Claudia off to another man. Evan shrugged mentally; he was too old to be nettled, his masculinity challenged. Or was he?

Clementine slipped her hand through his arm and stood beside him as though she did it every day. Evan started. She looked up at him, her eyes bright with happiness and excitement, her cheeks flushed with cold. He noted the soft line of her lips and ached to kiss her again. ''Tell me about the cows, Evan. What are their names? Oh, Evan, will there be calves this spring? Oh, I hope so. I love babies of any kind.''

Evan swallowed slowly and knew that if ever a woman needed babies to cuddle, it was Clementine Barlow.

He moved away from her slightly to pour the pellets into the trough. An eon ago, he'd wanted children and the years had dimmed the memory. He'd thought of a child with Claudia because he wanted the Tanner blood to hold the land.

He looked at Clementine warily. Jack Barlow and Claudia had misnamed the "little do-gooder." *She was certified female trouble.*

She listened carefully while he pointed out the cattle and their names. Clementine stroked a white-faced Hereford's back. The heifer had been disowned by her mother at birth. She had for a time considered Evan to be her mother, especially after the nights he lay close to her in the barn. "I think we should get milking cows, Evan," she said slowly as though considering a new concept. "That way we can offer fresh cream and butter to our guests, and they can have the experience of milking."

"Have you ever milked a cow, Clementine?"

She touched her beret and her eyes locked with his. "No, but I'm willing to learn. I want a cow to milk, Evan," she said distinctly. "One with pretty eyes."

That evening, Evan sat in the kitchen, trying to concentrate on the new crossword puzzle he had begun in order to forage mental privacy from Clementine and her loose-cannon ideas. Concentration wasn't easy when bedtime was nearing and Clementine would be settling upon the creaking old bedsprings upstairs.

The whole living-with-Clementine environment was unnatural to him. Evan shifted uneasily in his chair. As she cooked, she moved around the kitchen, a symphony of curves and sweet flesh and scents, and she thought he was sexually impaired.

He glared at the object of his dark thoughts. With very little effort, Evan could easily prove to her and to himself that—

"...We could see if that old mine would be the right environment to grow mushrooms. At first I thought the root cellar would be good for mushrooms, but I really want to keep canning jars and fruit there. If the mushrooms are successful, we can market them as fresh or pickled. And what about the blackberry bushes...women have always loved to make jams and I know our lady guests would just love the experience of canning on this old stove just like their great-grandmothers... Evan, are you listening?'' She carried a plate of deliciously browned chicken to the table.

"Haven't I been listening all day?" he grumbled as she sat down. He glanced warily at the warmed apple dumplings on the stove. They were a tasty temptation he could not afford.

Clementine smiled tightly and lifted her chin. "Don't be averse to new ideas, Evan. I just want to add to what you've begun so nicely. By the way, where's the washer and dryer?"

Evan filled in two more words on the puzzle before he answered, "There's the washtub and there's the clothesline running next to Big Bertha... a washer and a dryer." Then he smiled as Clementine's eyes widened.

She frowned at him. "You love to do that, don't you? Point out that life is primitive here? If you think that will discourage me, Mr. oh-so-smart-Evan Tanner, you are very mistaken. Shall we eat?"

She glanced down at the puzzle he had been working and pointed to the last missing block of letters. "Arrogant."

Evan saw instantly that the word fit into the puzzle. He inhaled sharply. His puzzles were his way of relaxing and Ms. Clementine Barlow had gone too far, stepping into them too easily and polishing off the last word. She was in his territory now. She was out of line. He could finish his crossword puzzles and anything else he started.

Later, while seated at the computer upstairs, Clementine said, "...A catalog sales business—the mushrooms and jams and candles from beeswax...and a Native American outlet shop would be just perfect for those take-home trinkets.''

All he had to do was wait until she discovered that she was not suited for roughing it. According to Jack Barlow, Clementine had grown up in the city; her discovery that she was not suited to primitive rural life should only be a matter of days. Less than a week, if Evan was lucky. He glanced at the clutter of feminine toiletries on his dresser and the huge plant, which occupied the window light near the computer. Jethro was already sending out explorative little runners to overtake the windowsill just as Clementine was invading Evan's life. Framed pictures of the Barlow clan, including Claudia and the boys, hung from the wall, and his usually neat desktop was filled with pottery mugs jammed with pencils and paper clips. Hippopotamus bookends dressed in ballerina tutus supported Evan's files. A hot-pink sewing box perched on the shelf with his boxes of rifle shells.

Evan groaned mentally, refusing to look at the disturbing froth of freshly washed lacy bras and briefs running across the old bed, which Clementine had opened to absorb the warmth of the room.

The cot that Clementine had made up for him next to Big Bertha was very unappealing after his role of Buddy-Bear.

''...If I just had a sewing machine...There's an old tablecloth that would be perfect for the kitchen windows. Oh, nothing fancy, just a ruffle across the top...I really think that behind the saloon, near that old orchard, would make a lovely place for a garden. It would be just off the kitchen and the guests might enjoy cooking on an outside stove—pioneers used to do that, you know. Then if you could make some window boxes, salmon-colored impatiens would be just beautiful against the weathered gray siding. Daisies along the front porch...and a climbing trellis for roses. The roses are so beautiful here that we'll want a rose garden, of course. The potpourri and sachets will be wonderful...and the house specialty dish shouldn't be beef. Something that's garden-fresh and has home-made pasta, I think—''

"What?" Evan asked, awash in a mind-bog of ruffled curtains, flowers and main dishes that weren't beef.

"Don't worry, Evan. I'll start the flowers from seed that I brought with me and I have friends in the garden-ing business who would be happy to send rosebushes. We'll want to grow our own pumpkins, too—'' She jot-ted a note.

"This is a guest ranch, not a florist shop or a grow-your-own eatery, Clementine," Evan stated very care-fully and suddenly realized he was gritting his back teeth and his fingers were lodged into his thighs. He had the breathless sensation of being roped, bulldogged and thrown to the ground. He could just see Clementine's red boot braced on his backside, pinning him in the dust. "Male guests like to rope and ride, maybe hunt and fish. You are not changing the Barlow Guest Ranch into a priss palace."

She turned to him and smiled tightly, a signal Evan had begun to realize preceded her sinking her heels into an idea and refusing to budge. A delicate eyebrow lifted and quivered just once. "No need to yell, Evan."

"Yelling?" he demanded in a soft roar because he had never shouted in his lifetime.

She frowned slightly, thoughtfully. "Claudia said you're usually very quiet until you have something to say. I specifically remember her saying that you were a quiet man. Are you feeling all right?"

"Fine," he said, glaring at her. He didn't want her prowling through his illnesses any more than he wanted her examining his suspected sexual malfunctions. She looked as though she was just a step away from feeling his forehead, blowing his nose and tucking him into bed. He wanted his life back, without the tutu-wearing, hippopotamuses bookends and the distracting lacy underwear covering a bed that had creaked with thousands of lovemaking sessions. He resented his body telling him that lovemaking with Clementine could disprove her theories. Because he was off-balance, Evan lashed out at her. "Don't even think about flowering the place up."

"We're not going to be rigid in our thinking, are we?" she asked tightly. "New ideas never hurt . . . and women do like to putter in gardens . . . men like gardening, too."

"Women." Evan bit out the word. "The Barlow Guest Ranch is set up for men. An outside shower without bubble bath. The house specialty is one-inch thick beefsteak and fried potatoes."

"Times change," Clementine shot back.

They stared at each other for a full five seconds, then Clementine smiled and straightened her shoulders. "I really don't want to pull rank on you, Evan. But if I must get you to see the logic of accommodating women and considering investing our profit in a ranch for needy, troubled girls as well as boys, I will. The Barlow Guest Ranch shouldn't be sexually biased."

"Uh-huh, I was waiting for that," he returned darkly. "I'd buy you out if I could. But I can't and I'm not leaving you to Tanner land."

"So you're stuck with me, aren't you?" she asked cheerfully, though her eyes challenged him.

"Right, boss." Evan cherished the dark glare she gave him before she turned back to the computer. He flipped his magazine to a fresh crossword puzzle and forced himself to concentrate on it.

All he had to do was to wait....

Clementine continued to jab at the computer and make frustrated noises, distracting Evan. He glanced at the screen, lunged to his feet and pushed the button that would retrieve the program that she wanted. "Thank you," Clementine said primly. "Electronics have never liked me."

Evan smirked down at her, then retreated to the safety of his new crossword puzzle.

After a half hour and a round of neatly placed financial questions, Clementine rose to her feet. She lifted her arms over her head and began a series of stretches that instantly drew Evan's concentration from his puzzle. His mouth dried. He was unable to move or look away. His body ached for the soft heat flowing in front of him.

Then Clementine leveled a sympathetic look at him. "You've been brooding about failing the tests all day, Evan. Once you accept that there is a problem, you'll realize that you really didn't suit Claudia...she's... well...she's rather highly sexual. Both of you would have been miserable. Usually, when a bride says no, it's for the best. Women can sense when their choice of a life mate is just a little off the mark—"

Evan inhaled slowly for about the fiftieth time that day. After watching Clementine's curved body arch and stretch, her full breasts thrusting at her sweater, and the mention of sexuality, he felt raw and needing. "As I understand it, those weren't 'tests,' they were magazine quizzes.... Clementine, if you say one more thing about my dysfunctional sexuality—"

"I'll help you to understand. I honestly did come to rescue you, Evan. I want to help erase the damage my family has done to yours. According to the papers I found in my father's old trunk, the Tanner's bad luck began when my grandmother jilted your grandfather. He married too quickly, just to show her that one bride was as good as another. Though his wife bore his children, she made his life miserable. No wonder he drank so." She stroked his hair, smoothing the crisp, black strands as Evan realized that he could not move away.

Instead, he reacted instinctively—wrapping his fingers around her wrist and jerking her into his lap.

After a soft gasp of surprise, Clementine sat very still. They stared at each other and Evan's hand opened to span and smooth the round curve of her hip. He wondered distantly when he had ever claimed a woman as abruptly, or desired anyone as much. He remembered the buttery, cinnamony delicious dumplings and knew that Clementine would taste a thousand percent better. Then Clementine continued stroking his hair. She hugged him and kissed his cheek. "There...there...I know this must be difficult. You're off-balance with this new knowledge and very emotional...for you. This can't be easy, Evan. When you're ready, I'll show you the series of magazine tests that proved you and Claudia weren't compatible ... ah ... sexually."

Evan blinked and wondered when his heart would start beating again. Then very carefully, he placed his lips over Clementine's.

When he lifted his head, Clementine's eyes slowly opened. She cleared her throat and flushed. "You're ... ah ... doing much better at expressing your emotions."

Evan realized that her fingers were digging into his shoulders and that her body was very, very soft. She quivered against him just once and he felt like grinning, an unfamiliar happy little warmth growing inside him. He circled his emotions mentally, nudging the tiny delightful glow. He didn't trust it. "How would you know?"

She flushed again. "Well...I...have been married, you know. And engaged."

"Then you must know that a man doesn't like his masculinity given a low rating."

"I said I would help you to understand your problem."

"And you don't have a problem?"

She blinked, surprised by his question. "Me? No, of course not."

Evan inhaled, allowing his chest to brush against her softness. He ran his hand down the curve of her hip and stroked the back of her knee beneath her jeans. Clementine stirred restlessly, her eyes flickering away from him. "It's natural for you to want to experiment, Evan. But you can let me up now."

Evan slid his fingers through the hair that was warm and scented of her. He lifted it to his nose and smelled deeply. He smiled into the silky strands. "Clementine, I've been wondering if you'd mind opening your lips and let me kiss you. Just to test my...problem. And yours."

She squirmed on his lap and looked at his mouth uncertainly. "Claudia said you never tried to make love with her. She said your kisses were brotherly. That you weren't an overheater or a steamer. She waited for just one session of breathing hard. Or hot, flushed skin...or something...some pressure against her...somewhere."

She frowned and squirmed again, easing her hips more fully over his thigh.

Evan rubbed his cheek against her soft one, enjoying the feel of her near him. "I'm not feeling brotherly now, Clemmie."

"You're just worked up because you're hurting about Claudia's decision, and you've begun realizing there is a problem. You've been challenged in a way you want to rebel against... You see, the male ego... Oh, very well," she said in a resigned, sacrificial tone. "Kiss me. You'll see. I've never been an overheater and you'll see that there is a problem."

When he looked down at her, Evan smiled. Clementine had puckered up and closed her eyes, waiting for him. A little shaft of joy went soaring through him, a tender warming that eased the coldness of the years. "I hope this experiment won't ruin me completely, Clemmie," he whispered before lowering his lips to hers.

Clementine allowed the soft brush-brush of Evan's mouth across hers. She grasped his hard shoulders to keep her mind from whirling away on a soft satiny cloud as he continued to nibble and forage on her lips, parting them slightly with the tip of his tongue. The texture of his new beard excited her, contrasting with the smooth seeking of his lips. He nuzzled and brushed and nibbled and tested until she sighed and snuggled closer to him. This magnificent, wounded creature was hers to tend, hers to shelter and to heal. She ached for his loneliness, for the hurt that he had suffered when Claudia chose another man.

She knew the exact depth of his pain, the emptiness when a marriage goes wrong, the deep insecurities caused by a broken engagement.

Clementine ran her hands over Evan's tense shoulders, and stroked his taut neck, enjoying the hard slide of muscle beneath his skin.

She sighed again and tasted Evan on her lips. There was an excitement lurking in his taste, one that she had never experienced. Hungry for the dark flavor, Clementine arched against him, pressed herself to the source of her delight and gently, daringly suckled the tip of his tongue. Evan inhaled sharply. With a hungry low groan deep in his throat, he gathered her to him firmly, and smoothed her bottom with his large palm. He squeezed lightly as if treasuring her. The claiming was seductive and luxurious, as if he would take all the time she needed. As if he was tasting her with his hands and finding her very delicious. Clementine cherished the intimate caress, allowing him to shift her body slightly as he continued to stroke and to soothe the restless ache that had begun within her.

She realized that Evan had slid to the floor, spreading her gently over him. In the distance, he murmured, a deep uneven tone filled with pleasure; he moved and she held him tighter, unwilling to let him leave her.

She lay over him, pressing him to the floor with the weight of her body, capturing his face with her hands. She kissed him with the fever that was riding her and ran her hands across his chest, resenting the western shirt keeping her away from him. Unable to resist, with a cry Clementine locked her arms around his neck and pressed her aching, sensitive breasts down upon him. They met the hard plane of his chest and the ache settled slightly, as if soothed.

Evan was very warm, breathing unevenly. Then he jerked up her sweater to caress her back.

Clementine arched against his hand, moving on him as he stroked down, then up her spine, gently massaging the muscles at the back of her neck. She wiggled closer, straddled him to keep him near, and cried out softly as his hand slid to cradle and caress her breast. "Oh, yes…Evan…yes," she heard herself whisper fiercely as the delicate tingles grew and caught her up in pleasure.

She rocked against him, speared her fingers through his hair and held his mouth against her seeking one.

The dark, wild taste fed her hunger and Clementine sighed, moving her body against his hardened one.

She wanted closer to the heat, closer to the tender hunger that was Evan— "Clementine?" he asked unevenly against her ear as she wiggled closer.

She stilled, aware that she had flattened Evan to the floor.

"Clementine?" He stroked her back, his big hands trembling, and Clementine shuddered, becoming shockingly aware of how she had taken advantage of Evan's emotional distress.

She breathed slowly, forcing air into her lungs and trying to force her body to separate from his. She took inventory of her body, willing it to respond. Delicate little tingles flowed through her thighs where they rested along his hard ones. Layers of their jeans separated Evan's apparent need from her intimate warmth.

One by one, she forced her fingers to unlatch from his shoulders.

She had been married and had made love. She blinked. Her ex-husband's clinical lovemaking had never evoked the tropical heat and fierce need that Evan had with a few kisses.

James had not touched her as if cherishing her like fine china, or warm silk. Yet Evan's calloused hands had caressed her leisurely as if he really enjoyed holding her.

As if her body delighted him.

As if he was hungry for the taste of her. As if he wanted to nibble and lick and kiss every inch of her.

Clementine shivered. Evan's steamy kisses certainly paled Morris's damp, fish-mouth ones. Evan's kisses told her he was a man who knew what he wanted. How to slant his mouth over a woman's and treasure her into delight.

Clementine sat up, pushed her hair from her flushed face and looked down at Evan. He looked drop-dead gorgeous, all-male. His hair was peaked by her restless fingers, his shirt opened slightly to reveal the hair on his chest. Her fingers twitched and she realized how badly she wanted to stroke his chest—his magnificent chest. Evan's mouth curved in a wistful, almost boyishly lopsided smile, then he lifted his hips gently against her. Once. Twice. A tentative movement that caused her thighs to tighten against him.

Then she realized that she was straddling him like a wrestler, pinning her opponent to the mat.

Zip and Slide plopped down near Evan's head, witnesses to her guilt.

Evan caught her trembling hand on its way to cover her "Oh!" and brought it to his lips. "Thank you, Clemmie. I see now that I do have a definite problem," he said in a dark, raspy tone.

Aghast with the sensuality that had stormed out of her, Clementine shook her head. "Oh, Evan . . . I am so sorry that I took advantage of you. This must be very painful for you."

"Oh, it is, Clementine," he whispered gently against her palm. When she frowned worriedly, afraid that she had damaged him beyond his old wounds, Evan's eyes widened slightly with something that looked like fear. A strand of black hair spearing over his forehead quivered. "Just don't hug me, Clementine. Not now."

Clementine flopped over on her stomach and the old bed creaked. She grabbed a pillow and jammed it close to her aching body. On the floor beside her, Zip whined questioningly and Slide snorted.

She flopped to her back, drawing the pillow on top of her stomach, and the bed creaked again.

James's real love had been his stamp collection. He'd made love to Clementine in the same systematic way that he'd placed stamps in a collector's book. She frowned. After sampling Evan's hungry, heated kisses, even though he was just experimenting with his sexuality, James's lovemaking reminded her of being stamped: "Bill Paid... Due Again Next Month."

Her frown darkened as she remembered James crooning and licking his stamps. He'd never kissed her with that enthusiasm. But to be fair, she had never straddled another man, either. James liked infinite, meticulous order to his life and his lovemaking. To James, sensually hungry women pinning submissive men beneath them was just not conventional.

After James's mother reclaimed him, Clementine had dealt with the pain of a failed marriage: What had she done? What hadn't she done?

Her answers to a quiz in the back of a ladies' magazine—"Are You Red-Hot?"—had given her the answer. She simply wasn't a woman that made men heat and steam. That knowledge had hurt for a time, deepened by Morris and his secretary's writhing across his desktop.

Clementine shuddered. Morris's kisses were always so damp.... She'd tried to vamp him once and the result had proved embarrassing—Morris had gone home to change his trousers. He was never quite the same after that.

She listened to the old hotel settling in... to Big Bertha moaning luridly downstairs. Evan had taken her wrist and tugged her into his lap. The dark excitement in his smoky eyes had caught her off guard. Though he was testing his sensuality, he touched her as if claiming her—as if no other man would take her away from him.

Clementine reached up and gripped the iron bars of the bed. She straightened out her body and pointed her toes, trying to exorcise the tension humming through her. She would have to start looking for magazine quizzes about women taking what they wanted. She would analyze the slant of her handwriting and just how she crossed her t's to better understand her actions. Somehow, the aggressive, greedy woman buried in her had surfaced when Evan kissed her. She had frightened Evan. He was afraid of her. His body had actually shuddered when he thought she was going to hug him.

Evan needed hugs, Clementine decided, pressing her thighs together until they quivered beneath the thermal cloth. Then she remembered how she had straddled him, pinned him to the floor, and she forced her legs to relax. The unaccountable sensitivity in her breasts was almost painful as she thought about the planes of Evan's warm, hard chest.

She crossed her legs and ignored the unusual tingling, aching sensation.

And just for a moment, she had forgotten his wounds and his delicate psyche. Evan had suffered too much already and she had attacked him, very likely deepening his wounds.

Clementine gripped the bars of the old bed tighter. If ever she wanted to dive on top of a man, experience the wild heat and fire and lightning that the questionnaires said existed in truly sensual, fulfilling relationships, it was when she had captured Evan on the floor. Poor man. He was probably shocked, dealing with his problems now as he lay next to Big Bertha. Trying to soothe him now might only frighten him more. Clearly, he was still aching from Claudia's jilting of him.

Clementine yawned and snuggled down with the pillow. She hadn't realized how much she missed Buddy-Bear until now.

Evan slammed the nail with his hammer, unlocking all the force of his emotions. Mosey had ventilated the barn wall again, loosening five boards that kept the cold wind from the stock. After listening to Clementine's bed creak for an hour, Evan welcomed the familiar thud of Mosey's hooves against the barn boards. He welcomed the cold mist stinging his flushed skin and the therapeutic repair of the old barn. Anything was better than lying next to Big Bertha's moaning and listening to that old well-used bed creak with the weight of Clementine's delectable buttery-warm curves. About a hundred years ago, the taut edge of desire had ridden him like this, though Evan didn't remember the poignant ache being quite as sharp.

Back then, he'd wanted fulfillment for his body alone. But kissing Clementine was a hunger that he was certain he'd want to sample more than once. He had the uneasy feeling that he would enjoy talking to Clementine about things that didn't matter—like the tutu-clad hippopotamuses.

He jerked off his glove, tipped back his hat and rubbed the dull ache across his forehead. His hand smelled like the liniment he'd used to warm Mosey's back legs and ease the pain brought on by his kicking fit. Evan allowed his eyes to lift to the upper-story window where Clementine slept.

He inhaled slowly, remembering Clementine's body riding his. The fierce, hungry exhilaration that shimmered from her, enveloping him in a sweet, tender cloud, had startled him at first.

Clementine Barlow's kisses tasted like her apple dumplings, warm and buttery and spiced with a sharp exciting sense that she would taste better every time he went back for another helping.

He wondered darkly where she kept those questionnaires about sexuality. There had to be some answers about a man feeling like one big grin and half his age when a woman came after him. When she snared him with soft arms and legs and pinned him beneath her and kissed him as if she could dive in and wallow in him and cherish and love him.

Love. Evan inhaled the sharp, cold mist swirling around him.

There would be none of that in his life. He wasn't up to that particular weakness or the pain it brought.

Five
***

Evan awoke to the sound of hushed whispering and the symphony of the greyhounds' paws hitting the stairway's boards. He lay still on the cot and opened one eye. Judging by the morning light invading the saloon, he knew that he had slept past his usual waking hour and that the time was near seven o'clock.

Clementine continued to hush and soothe and the greyhounds quieted. Evan angled his head to view the stairway just as Clementine's denim-clad bottom settled gently on the old oak banister. She wiggled slightly as if testing the strength of the wood. There was a flash of red boots as she slid down to the bottom and hopped off with a victorious grin. She patted the greyhounds, who rubbed against her.

Zip's and Slide's smooth coats were covered with what looked like the pieces of an old blanket. When Clementine opened the door, they bounded out of the hotel. She went to the large, curtainless windows and placed her hands low on the sill, bending to watch the greyhounds outside.

The view of Clementine's curved backside did not help the tension that had been running through Evan since she'd pinned him to the floor. He inhaled stealthily as she stood on tiptoe, stretched and touched the toes of her boots several times.

When she turned to him, Evan closed his eyes and waited. Her footsteps came nearer until she stood beside him. He forced himself to breathe slowly as her scent flowed around him. A soft hand gently smoothed back the strand of hair crossing his forehead. Then carefully, slowly, Clementine eased Evan's hands beneath the blankets as she pulled them up to cover his bare shoulders. She patted his chest once, the gesture smacking of motherly comfort.

Evan lay very still as he listened to her footsteps crossing to the kitchen.

At forty-two, he had just been tucked into bed by a woman he wanted to draw into it.

He opened his eyes to the ceiling and knew without a doubt that Clementine Barlow was dangerous. She'd winded him with the tender gesture as surely as if he'd been bucked off a Brahman bull.

A week later, Evan tried to ignore the mouth-watering aroma of baking apple pies as he entered the office. Clementine looked up from the photographs and clippings that she had pasted to sheets of paper. She studied the arrangement and jotted a note. "Maud said that this would do for a start. She can develop a brochure for the Barlow ranch in less than a week, and once we okay it, she'll trade the printing expenses for going on a genuine cattle drive.

She's especially interested in doing rope tricks like Will Rogers—ones where she can hop in and out of the loop.... Do you know anyone who could teach her, Evan?''

After nights without sleep, kept awake by sounds of Clementine's bed creaking, Evan wasn't in the mood to shop for a rope-trick tutor. He wasn't happy to discover that he had been deliberately lingering in bed in the mornings, waiting for Clementine's bottom to slide down the banister . . . and waiting for her to pull up his blanket.

This morning, she'd paused before drawing up the blanket and for just a moment, Evan sensed that she was considering placing her hand over his chest. If she had, she would have discovered his racing heartbeat.

"Lucky Wallace might do it. He helped keep the men in their saddles at the roundup last year. But Clementine, we haven't exactly settled the matter of women guests."

"Bartering is an age-old method of settling debts. We do need those brochures, Evan. Maud is a top-notch lay-out artist with her own printing company and she's a good athlete."

"Last year, one guest said he could handle everything the machines at his gym could offer. He had to be helped into his bedroll the first night of the drive." Evan glanced at the strips of old cloth that Clementine was braiding into a rug. This room was looking too homey. He felt vaguely uncomfortable and nettled because it was *his* office. "Last year, I had more applications than there were saddles."

She considered his input and grinned. "Then we'll up the price of the vacations. By the way, I think we should add a wood-chopping contest—the person who chops the most firewood wins extra days—that way, we'll have our winter firewood for Big Bertha. The guests will like the exercise and the competition."

Evan weighed the thought and nodded reluctantly. Clementine's business intuitions were inventive and sound. He'd survived Clementine's feminine scents whirling around him at every turn. He'd survived tantalizing pasta-based meals, topped with her encouraging tidbits to "let it all out," and a slathering of "opening up is good for the soul." He'd survived a day spent with Clementine riding over the ranch, explaining the route that the cattle drive would take, circling the ranch's perimeter and the various camps. He'd managed another day answering questions about the guests' accommodations, which were "bring your own bedroll and camping gear." That afternoon, the chinook—a warm wind—had melted the snow and Clementine had been delighted to explore the property behind the house, which included the new well, the root cellar and a junkyard.

Wearing Evan's galoshes over her red boots and dressed in her beret and maxicoat, she had tromped around the ancient trash, delighted to extract two old coffee jars, which she had washed lovingly. The first of many she hoped to retrieve, they stood on the kitchen counter filled with coffee and sugar. A collection of old patent-medicine bottles was soaking in a metal dishpan, and spread on a tarp on the saloon floor was an assortment of old hand tools and enameled pots. Turn-of-the-century litter covered the floor at one end of the saloon. When she could, Clementine planned to forage and clean the entire mound of discarded, antique trash. Apparently, the flowers she wanted splashed around and in the hotel would look great in chipped commodes and enamel cooking pots.

While polishing the dark wood of the saloon's long bar and chattering about an old recipe for furniture polish using beeswax and lemon, Clementine had discovered the ten-foot-long painted reclining figure of Miss Matilda

Dryer. Clementine's mouth had parted and closed repeatedly as she stared at the buxom woman draped in a sheer swathe of cloth that only covered her navel. Clementine had immediately placed a sheet over Matilda's inviting, sensuous smile and her lushly endowed, pale body. She had turned to Evan, who managed to meet her dark frown with an innocent expression. "No," she had said in a tight, furious voice before marching into the kitchen.

"Yes," Evan had murmured, because if there was anything Clementine was not changing in her short stay, it was Matilda. She had been his companion through one or two dark moments and he had treasured her from the moment he found her standing upright and dusty behind a stack of boards. Last summer's round of guests had also loved her and she had been enthusiastically toasted in their final celebration.

Clementine had returned from the kitchen instantly. "You've done a wonderful job of restoring the bar, Evan. The wood is beautiful. But...she—" she waved her hand at the woman reclining on the floor behind the bar "—she has to go. Looking at her isn't good for your...problem. Dressed like that—looking like that, and that expression on her face—as if she's..." Clementine cleared her throat as a flush rose to heat her cheeks. "That picture will only hurt you. It will remind you of your— It's for your own good."

Evan had tossed his hat to the cot and looked steadily at her. "Matilda stays," he said, meaning it.

Clementine's finely arched left eyebrow had lifted and quivered before her lips had tightened. Evan watched with interest as she gathered herself for another approach. She had smiled in her sympathetic, I-know-I-know way and said, "We'll talk about it later. You don't appear to be in a receptive mood right now, Evan. Not very flexible at all.''

Evan's thoughts had turned over the statement as he watched Clementine's hips sway on her way back into the kitchen. It was true that he felt very rigid.

Therefore he'd spent that afternoon out riding fences and repairing the barbed wire, which had been cut. The footprints in the mud near the severed wire led to the all-terrain tire tracks that soared up a hill, which had challenged the skills of the driver. Evan knew that hill; he'd walked and ridden it enough on his way to the cabin where his father died. When he'd made the bargain with Jack Barlow, Evan had returned to that cabin hidden in the pines. It was just as cold as ever, filled with memories that sliced through him as though they were yesterday.

The cot that he'd slept on was still there, and the one that his father had wasted away upon.

He scanned the deep ruts of the four-wheel-drive vehicle and wondered if the newcomer had spotted the cabin. The sloping hill bore muddy trails around the sagebrush. Whoever the mischief maker was, he had perched on a hill overlooking the hotel and had done so several times.

Evan disliked the thought of someone spying on Clementine even more than uprighting the outhouse, which they'd found tipped over again while they rode over the ranch. The neatly stacked pipes that would be used to connect the well to the house and for the new sewer had been disturbed. The mischief was irritating more than harmful; Evan had noted the footprints around the pipe matched those on the hill overlooking the house.

Another irritation was the ease with which Clementine could polish off a crossword puzzle.

'' . . . Maud thinks the guest ranch with a cattle drive is a wonderful Americana experience. The mock branding disturbs her, though, even when I told her it was done with red paint,'' Clementine was saying as Evan sat in front of the computer and began typing. He tried to ignore the pink tutu of the hippopotamus nearest him. Clementine studied the screen with interest. ''Evan, what are you doing?''

He was trying not to think about women flowering the place up, about geraniums growing out of porcelain pots which had once been placed under beds. The old table beneath a window of the saloon held a variety of old cans containing dirt. Neatly aligned to catch the sun and monitored morning and night by Clementine, the hundred or so cans forebode a wealth of flowers and herbs. Several packages of seeds and mushroom spores rested beside them.

Evan almost regretted that Clementine would not see the seeds spring into life.

He longed to hang Matilda on the wall and stare at her and remember Clementine's flushed face as she straddled him. The memory of her little hungry purrs and her nails pressing into his shoulders as they kissed was a tidbit that wouldn't be pushed away, nor the nightly sound of the old bed creaking with her weight.

He'd found himself envying a stuffed toy called Buddy-Bear. Evan scowled at the computer screen; whimsy never had fit into his life and he pushed it away.

''I'm sending a message to Mark Livingston. Telling him to let Old Spot and Missie out. They're old draft horses and he's been keeping them for the winter because the barn isn't big enough. They'd been staying here for years before I arrived. They'll come on home once Mark releases them. They'll need shoeing. Mark said he'd help me with the plumbing and now would be a good time for that, too. I helped him bale hay last year and add a room onto his house.''

"I see. Bartering is a good way to help each other," Clementine said thoughtfully.

She knelt by his side, placed her hand on his knee and watched quietly while Evan sent a computer message to John White requesting twenty horses and saddles in another month. He ordered grain from Bill Johns and requested a delivery to Loomis and tried to ignore the freshly washed scent of Clementine's hair and her pale fingers gripping his thigh.

When he finished sending his messages, Clementine looked up at him with a delighted expression. "How wonderful—cowboys going electronic!"

Very little kept Evan from reaching down, placing his hands along her cheeks and drawing her up into his kiss.

Clementine's eyes widened and her left eyebrow quivered. She looked at his mouth, then up to his eyes. "Oh, Evan," she whispered softly. "You'll see. Everything is for the best.... If you would just open up to me, I could help you."

Evan thought of ways she could help him. He ached in every tense muscle and he longed desperately for one of Clementine's sweet, cinnamony kisses.

The knowledge that he wanted her more than he wanted his solitude and peace went sailing through him.

He'd been comfortable with Claudia and nettled by her choosing another man. He would have preferred to keep his thoughts private and not have them probed by a do-gooder who excited him.

Evan stood slowly, looking down at Clementine, and counted the steps to the old bed, still warm and rumpled from her nap. Zip and Slide lifted their heads as if sensing the vibrations trembling between Evan and Clementine.

Evan's mouth tightened grimly. Of course, Clementine wasn't aware of how much he wanted her. He breathed unsteadily, nodded and left the room before he told her how he really didn't want to barter with Maud.

He also left before he gave in to the temptation to kiss Clementine's softly parted mouth, recently moistened by the enticing, nervous flick of her tongue.

Clementine jumped to her feet the moment Evan slammed the door behind him. She pressed her shaking hands to her throat, covering her racing pulse. In another moment, she would have grabbed Evan and— She swallowed tightly. Evan's smoky eyes had darkened warily as their eyes locked.

He couldn't know how she longed for one of his sweet kisses, the brush-brush of his lips on hers, tantalizing her. How she longed to snuggle against him and hold him, kiss that tiny vein that raised along his temple when he was concentrating on his crossword puzzles or when he was resisting opening up to her help to resolve his loss of Claudia.

On his cot every morning, Evan's chest was tanned against the white sheets and absolutely beautiful with its wedge of black hair curling just up to the base of his throat. He was considering the question of his sexual dysfunction now; he was too quiet and brooding when she brought up the subject to him. The tiny little vein started throbbing immediately when Clementine entered the area of his sexuality.

She sighed and petted Zip's and Slide's smooth heads. While Evan looked as if he wanted to test her theories, he still wasn't very receptive to invasion in this part of his life. She stood, listening to the steady tramp of his boots back up the stairs. The door opened and Evan walked through it. He walked to her. "I'm a little tired of your amateur psychology, Clemmie," he stated darkly.

She backed up a step, but refused to be intimidated. "I'm trying to help—"

Evan cupped her chin with his hand, forcing her to look up at him. "I know...you want to rescue me... Okay, Clemmie, you're into bartering—here's my deal. I'll consider your dingbat theories if you tell me about your exhusband and about your fiancé. It seems to me that you're carrying a little excess baggage yourself."

"I've dealt with my problems and I understand myself," she said slowly, warily as Evan bent nearer.

He smelled so good.

"Is that so?" he asked in a husky drawl. "So you've taken all these magazine tests and they told you exactly what your problems were, and then you dealt with them. Is that right?"

She looked away to the two greyhounds who were watching with interest. It seemed only fair to tell Evan the truth. Her cheeks burned as she sorted through her thoughts. "I've never been...the sort of woman men drool over. I recognized that fact on my wedding night."

"Uh-huh." He looked at her mouth and she wished her bottom lip would stop quivering. Evan's long leg slid between hers, his hard thigh nudging her gently, intimately. "What happened?"

She shivered, unable to draw her eyes away from the smoky depths of his. His thigh moving against hers created sensations that weakened her legs. She cleared her throat, and Evan's thumb caressed the movement. "It's private."

"Uh-huh. I'll just bet it is. I've got a pretty good idea what happened. Well, take a note, Clemmie. My life is private, too. It will stay that way after you're gone. You'll be going soon enough, won't you?"

She blinked as Evan leaned closer, his thumb stroking her cheek. "It won't work, Clemmie," he said in a dark uneven tone and she noticed the tiny vein in his temple throbbing beneath the dark skin.

She managed to find her voice. A husky, breathless tone slid from her. She'd just discovered that her fingers had latched on to Evan's belt and very little kept her from jerking him to her. "What won't?"

"Whatever you've got planned. Despite the Barlow reins, this is Tanner land and I'm keeping it." Then he bent his head and took her lips in the gentlest, sweetest kiss she'd ever had.

He studied her later, his thigh nudging her gently, rhythmically and Clementine leaned back against the wall for support. "Ah . . . you wouldn't just now be realizing how you should have acted with Claudia, would you, Evan?" she asked unsteadily. "It's too late for that."

Evan nibbled on her ear and nuzzled her cheek. "Clemmie, your sister isn't on my mind."

"Oh. You probably just don't recognize—" She stopped talking when his thigh moved against her.

He breathed unevenly and moved his chest slowly, luxuriously against her breasts. "What do you want, Clemmie? Do you still want to rescue me?"

Minutes later, Clementine listened to the male voices downstairs and wondered when she could unlaminate herself from the support of the wall. The dogs were whining at the door Evan had just closed behind him. She walked unsteadily to the door and when she opened it, the greyhounds bounded out of the room. Clementine gripped the old glass doorknob and a quiver ran down her legs as she remembered Evan's sweet, tender kiss and his thigh moving between hers. She touched her beret—of course, Evan was upset, but if he'd meant to intimidate her, he'd chosen the wrong woman. She jerked the door wider and walked down the stairs.

She wasn't leaving and she would not allow Evan to take out his frustrations and pain about Claudia on herself. She decided to tell him as much—

Evan and a boy about seventeen turned to look up at her. She hoped the shadows of the afternoon concealed the flush that covered her cheeks. She lifted her chin as Evan's gray eyes studied her face and the boy let out a long, low wolf whistle as she stepped off the last step. "Man, all this and she can cook, too? Way to go, dude. Maybe I'll see about staying here for vacation instead of going to Mom's. They're divorced. Dad is too busy to go anywhere and she's pretty well busy with her new family. Hanging around here could be okay," the boy said as Clementine smiled at him.

She refused to look at Evan, who continued to study her as he introduced Brent Young, a neighbor. Evan shifted his weight to one long leg as he looked at her mouth and Clementine realized that every nerve in her body wanted to leap on him or let him cuddle her. The thought thoroughly shocked her. Somehow she managed to offer Brent a slice of hot apple pie. "I want to talk to you when you finish eating, Brent," Evan said. Then he tugged the brim of his hat down in the standard western acknowledgment to women and walked outside.

Clementine resented Evan's leaving the battlefield, although she realized that Brent's presence did not allow for settling matters.

For the next two weeks, Evan and Mark Livingston worked on the plumbing and the well. Moving around Mark's six-foot-six, three-hundred-pound body did not seem as intimidating as Evan's lean frame when Clementine served as the little errand-fetcher, wrench-getter. When Clementine tried to begin a conversation with Mark, he seemed especially sensitive to Evan's dark stares. He did tell her he was married to "Old S.J."

She believed from Evan's grim expression that he was avoiding serious conversation with her. No doubt he was using the space she allowed him to think about the possibility of his therapy. She didn't understand the restless, edgy, primitive feeling that leapt on her when she thought about Evan's tender kisses. She searched for magazine interpretations of kisses and retook tests that she had failed when focusing on James and Morris. Her answers when considering Evan were different from her previous ones and she spent long hours missing Buddy-Bear in her creaking bed.

One long night after she had flip-flopped in the bed for hours, Evan had marched up the stairs and jerked the door shut with a fury that rattled the windows.

The old glass knob had plopped softly to the new braided rug she had made, and without thinking, Clementine leapt out of bed, jerked open the door and yelled down at Evan, "I need my sleep."

He had stood at the bottom of the stairs, his hands on his hips. His hair was tousled and he was wearing boxer shorts. He ran both hands through his hair and Clementine found herself saying very primly, "If you didn't have midnight conversations with Matilda, you might not be so grumpy."

"Matilda?" he had asked in a tone that resembled a bear's surly growl.

"You stare at her all the time. You must be in love."

In the dim light, his broad chest rose and fell as if he was taking deep, restraining breaths. He continued to look up at her for several seconds. Her breasts tingled beneath the old T-shirt of Evan's that she had discovered in her laundry. Her bare legs felt very . . . bare as he stood there, watching her. Then Evan had said warily, "I am moving to the barn."

"You'll catch cold. I won't be held responsible," she'd said and was met with silence while Evan ran his hands through his hair again, making it stand out in peaks.

She had stood at the top of the stairs and watched him toss clothing onto his cot and carry the whole affair out the front door, which he had slammed behind him.

Every night since he'd left, the hotel groaned its loneliness from every corner. Clementine pulled the blankets up to her chin and hoped the skunks or other creatures would not invade the stairway during the night.

Brent rode his horse to the ranch every two or three days and delivered the mail, which included letters from previous vacationers who wanted to return. Brent also brought the rest of her things, including Sissie, and nursery trees that had arrived at the post office. He seemed to enjoy purchasing fresh fruit and groceries for Clementine and beamed when she baked him special, extra-large cinnamon rolls.

Evan rose early now and she really missed tending his chest—covering it with the blankets. He'd reverted to the silent man Claudia had described, though there was a certain alert tightening to his body when Clementine was near and his eyes did darken when they looked at her mouth.

Several times, she had licked her lips, considering the idea that perhaps she had buttery crumbs clinging to them.

The first of May, Clementine had taken a luxurious bubble bath in one of the new shower-tubs that Evan and Mark had installed with the glorious extra-capacity hot-water heater. She had managed with the old galvanized tub and reveled in the new luxury of hot water that she didn't have to heat on the stove. When she had emerged, dressed in Evan's thermal underwear and her hair wrapped in a towel, Evan had met her smile with a dark scowl that had jerked down her body, then back up.

"If you think that will make a difference, you're wrong," he had muttered ominously. Then he had crushed the crossword puzzle he had been working into a ball, flung it into Big Bertha's cold belly and walked out of the hotel. She'd considered his obscure comment for hours while arranging a collection of old spurs on the hotel's board walls.

She had sat, cross-legged, studying the sun touching the cobalt blue medicine bottles in the window when she'd heard Evan behind her the next day. "What do you think, Evan? Aren't they great?" she had asked.

"Uh-huh...great," he had agreed flatly, and when she turned to offer him a friendly smile, Clementine's thoughts stopped.

She had been unable to look away from his body outlined by the bathroom light behind him. A lean, angular man, he was wearing white shaving cream over his jaw and a thin, worn towel around his hips. Later, she realized her hand ached from strangling the hammer she had been using. She tried to think of James's body and came up with a jellylike, pale midsection that draped over his belt.

Evan's midsection had a defining line of hair running down it and tight, molded muscles that shifted when he moved. When he had turned back to the bathroom, Clementine sucked in her breath. Covered by the thin cloth, Evan's hard backside flowed into long, beautiful legs.

The hammer had dropped when she remembered one of his thighs nudging her intimately.

She threw herself into gardening and when she walked to ease the tight feeling inside her, Mosey followed her. Clementine loved the old mule and knew that Evan babied him, despite grumbling that the animal was a worn-out old troublemaker.

Old beds of daffodils were sprouting in the backyard of the hotel and Clementine spent hours thinking of the ladies who must have enjoyed them. She loved the bottles she had gathered from the junkyard, and since the danger of frost had passed, she placed her assortment of potted herbs and flowers out in the sun. The collection of old two-man saws and broken files and rusty scythe blades set off a corner of the saloon. The various crocks and jars looked beautiful in the walk-in pantry.

Clementine steadfastly ignored Miss Matilda Dryer. When Evan had resolved his problems, she would approach him about evicting Matilda. She toyed with the idea that Evan might have a love-gone-wrong fixation on the lusty painting from the way he lifted the sheet every now and then and considered Matilda's curves the same way he contemplated freshly baked apple dumplings, which he loved.

Once Clementine had noted that Evan had an apple dumpling on his plate and had paused in the middle of spooning syrup over it. He'd rubbed the back of his spoon over the dumpling, circled it lovingly and then delved the tip of his spoon into the exact center. Clementine had watched in fascination while he licked the buttery cinnamon tidbit from his spoon with an intense expression. When he sensed she was looking at him, Evan's dark skin had flushed. "No, I will not take a test to determine anything," he had said firmly.

Clementine puttered around the room she had prepared for Cookie, which was next to the kitchen. Evan had said that climbing the stairs caused Cookie's hip problems to flare up and hadn't objected to the use of the small room. In another month, the guests would be arriving—twenty men of assorted ages who would place their bedrolls on the saloon floor when the weather did not permit sleeping outside. She hoped they liked her apple dumplings as Evan did.

There were times when she just wanted to hold Evan and when she wanted him to hold her in that marvelous, safe, tender way.

She realized from the moment that Evan kissed her and she had straddled him on the floor, that neither James nor Morris could excite her the way Evan did.

Nor infuriate her the way Evan did.

Nor kiss the way Evan did.

Six

Evan shifted in the saddle and scanned the cloudy, early-afternoon sky. On the trail behind him, Clementine rode the Appaloosa mare and tried to shoo Mosey back to the ranch. The old mule brayed soulfully and stopped each time Clementine looked back, then continued following them. A younger mule, which Evan had just purchased, took in the whole mule-tutoring process and doggedly followed Mosey. Evan allowed Pow-Wow the freedom because he wanted the younger mule to know his way back to the ranch. The pine-covered mountains, once mined for silver and gold, hugged the meadows, lush with deep grass. Sagebrush that would turn blue-gray in the summer grew beside creosote bushes. Meandering along a rocky ridge overlooking the meadow, an old wooden chute braced by boards had taken water to the miners and to the new orchards when the mining boom had finished.

Cookie was due to turn up any day, and in another month—the first of June—the guests would arrive. Clementine had reluctantly agreed to wait until she'd experienced the first round of guests before they reached a decision about opening the ranch to women vacationers. After all, she had never been on a cattle drive and realized that certain adjustments might have to be made for women guests. She had instantly suggested a portable, chemical toilet. She had insisted that it would not take up that much room in the chuck wagon, which would be pulled by the two mules.

Evan watched a hawk soar above the pine trees. Clementine's ideas, such as running the water from the outside shower stall down into the garden, had merit. The fresh vegetables and fruit would be a welcome addition to Cookie's meat-and-potato menu. The apple dumplings would make any guest want to return—Evan forced his thoughts away from the buttery delicacies that reminded him of Clementine's scent.

With each day, Evan's realization deepened that he wanted to show Clementine a part of his past—something that he had shared with no one else. For that reason, he had asked her to ride with him. Clementine had agreed softly, watching him carefully. "Yes, of course I'll go."

She hadn't questioned him about his destination; she had simply gotten a sweater and mounted the mare he had saddled.

Clementine was as Claudia had described her—trusting and gentle, ready to support and love without question.

She'd taken Brent under her wing, treating him to hot baked bread and butter and advice on how to treat girls. As Evan had asked, the teenager had been watching for the person causing the mischief and hadn't seen anything.

Brent's father gave him money, but not the time or attention the quiet youth needed. He seemed to like the task Evan had asked him to do, checking on the Barlow land as he passed. Lately, Brent was making it a point to ride to the old hotel to visit with Clementine, especially in the midmorning when she usually baked. It was obvious that Brent took the job seriously and hadn't informed Clementine that there might be problems, just as Evan had asked. It was also obvious that he adored Clementine and had shyly given her a pewter hippopotamus with a yawning mouth to hold pencils. When she had hugged him and kissed his cheek, Brent had blushed and had backed all the way out of the hotel.

Evan knew exactly how he felt, though he hadn't experienced any of those fast hugs and kisses lately.

He missed them.

Evan shifted restlessly in the saddle, feeling the cold seep into his bones, the way it did when he thought about his father. Ben Tanner had grown up in a bitter house, his mother flying at his alcoholic father for his failure—for marrying her and ruining her life. Ben had taken drinking and bitterness into his marriage, and Evan's mother had had enough by the time he was five years old. Until then, he'd known the safety of a child and the love of both parents.

The old cabin loomed up ahead of them, hidden by pine trees and sumac bushes. Clementine guided her horse next to his and Evan sensed her warmth and understanding. He reluctantly admitted that he wanted a little of her "do-gooder" care right now.

He jerked a hammer from his saddlebag and pried open the boards covering the door. The old lock was rusted, the key turning slowly. The door creaked open to the shadows of Evan's life. He walked into the cold, brushing away the cobwebs with a sweep of his hat.

"This is where you grew up after your mother died, isn't it, Evan?" Clementine asked softly beside him. Her hand touched his arm briefly, then wrapped it around his waist, anchoring him to her warmth and softness as the memories slammed against him.

He wanted to run away, just as he had done when he was a boy.

But he'd always come back.

Because Ben Tanner needed him in order to die.

Evan moved away from Clementine, unwilling to share the pain sweeping into him, tearing him apart. She waited as he walked slowly over the dusty, brittle linoleum of the single room to the rusting black stove. He jammed the tilted pipe back into place and looked at the cots that had been his father's and his own. The blankets were dry, though covered with dust. The plastic he'd placed over the old footlocker remained intact—filled with memories he couldn't open. In a corner, protected by a brace of boards, dust covered the plastic draped over the old sewing machine.

It had been Evan's grandmother's and his father had valued the black and gold-leaf machine, keeping it well oiled. It reminded him of when the Tanner homestead had sprawled across the Okanogan Valley land—a time before Jack Barlow had purchased the last acreage in the Tanner name. Evan lifted away the protective boards and drew back the thick layer of plastic. He slowly crouched beside the old machine, drew off his gloves and picked up the can of oil sitting on the ornate treadle. He eased it into the places Ned Tanner had carefully shown him, then placed his hand on the old treadle. The cold metal moved slowly beneath his hand, back and forth, the belt moving the sewing needle down and up—*click, click... click... click.*

Clementine's red boots gleamed in the dim light as she stood then knelt beside him. "It's beautiful, Evan."

He rubbed an oily cloth over the metal, protecting it against dampness. "My grandmother's machine. A wedding gift from my grandfather."

The agonizing pain and the cold years swirled around him, devouring him. "Evan?" Clementine's soft voice eased through the shadows.

Then she was holding him fiercely, her body pressed against him, a soft shield against his pain. "Evan," she whispered achingly against his throat and he felt the warmth of tears on her lashes.

Clementine had never seen such sadness, so much pain as when she looked at Evan. Grief rode the dark angles of his face as his hand opened to span the old treadle, moving it up and down slowly. She shuddered against him, feeling the cold pain surging out of him.

She held him tightly, refusing to allow him to draw back into the shadows as he tensed against her. She kissed his throat, placed her lips on the dark, throbbing pulse and soothed it as she stroked his taut neck.

"Clementine?" At Evan's deep voice, she hurled herself into his pain. Its fierce coldness terrified her. She fought the empty loneliness with her lips, opening them gently on Evan's mouth, kissing the hard contours gently.

Evan shuddered, his arms wrapping around her, jerking her closer as if he needed her to survive.

She held him as tightly, allowing no wedge of coldness to slide between them.

Evan's mouth slanted against her own, not the playful, seductive, teasing brush-brush she had known, but the hungry, desperate demand of a man needing a woman.

Clementine welcomed the pressure of his arms, the fierce spread of his hand against her back, the pressure of each finger claiming her. She wanted this, the hot desire flowing from him to her, the eager searching of his hand for her breast.

Buttons tore as Evan pushed up her sweater and ripped open her blouse, then he shuddered, looking down at the lace covering her breasts as if he were starved for her warmth. "Clementine . . ."

He shook his head as though dazed, his pain racing through the silvery shadows of his eyes. "I—"

"Don't you dare stop now, Evan Tanner," Clementine whispered before she pulled her sweater over her head. She met his frown with her determined one as she drew off his denim jacket. She spread it on the floor with her sweater. She jerked off her boots, tossed them aside and lay down, looking up at him. She obeyed her instincts to salve his past and to warm him, lifting her arms to welcome him.

"No," he whispered rawly, even as the trembling sweep of his open hand ran from her throat to her stomach and flattened over the gentle mound over her thighs. His long fingers curved into the material covering her femininity and he closed his eyes, as though seeking the will to push away her moist warmth.

"Yes," she returned softly as she tugged open the snaps of his western shirt and drew him gently over her. She wouldn't let him escape back to the past, not now, not when he needed her—

"Clementine," he whispered between hungry, hot kisses that trailed down to her breasts. He nudged aside the lace and silk, flicking the taut, aching nub with his tongue, then treasuring her other breast with the same tantalizing treatment.

"Clementine Rose," she whispered just as his hand tore away the cloth and his mouth opened on her breast, suckling it deeply.

Heat raced through Clementine, her hands sliding over his chest, smoothing the taut, shifting planes. She lifted her hips and Evan's long legs slid between hers, his hard body thrusting at hers as his hand reached between them to unzip her jeans. "You're so sweet...so warm...so soft," he whispered roughly against her skin as she melted, trembling, quivering around his stroking fingers.

Evan arched away slightly as he drew off her jeans. His gaze flicked down her body, the smoky shade of his eyes deepening as his dark hand claimed one pale breast, then the other, gently sweeping down to span her stomach and lower to cup her intimately. "You're ready for me, Clemmie," he whispered in a raw, amazed tone. "So hot and tight. You're making me burn."

"How nice," she said with pleasure, because she delighted in Evan's hunger for her. For just this moment, with this special, tender, wounded man, she wanted to open her body, clearing away his shadows and giving him life. But within her rose the selfish need to have him for her own, to claim him and make him hers. She touched him shyly, boldly, her fingers stroking the hard outline of his desire beneath the denim shielding him.

Evan's body tightened, his hand catching her seeking one and drawing it to his lips. Across their hands, his eyes promised, heated, desired—"Yes," she whispered to his silent question, her body arching against him, her legs holding his stronger ones prisoner.

His eyes closed, the harsh lines easing across his forehead and beside his mouth. "I'll take care of you," he whispered as she ran her trembling fingertips across his mouth—the lips she wanted taking hers in that fierce, hungry way as if nothing mattered but the loving between them, the deep needs met with each touch, each lingering gaze.

She moved against him, eager for his passion. "Love me, Evan. Take me. . . ."

Then Evan was shifting, and she protested his movement away from her as he drew out his wallet. His care to protect her only deepened her trust of him, deepened the tenderness she felt for him. A heartbeat later, he closed his eyes briefly, then opened them as she inhaled sharply against the strong, unfamiliar pressure. He shuddered, bracing his weight away as she adjusted to him, soothing her with kisses that gently seduced her from her fears.

Then Evan was truly hers, their bodies locked, and she claimed him with all her strength. His tall body rested on hers as Evan raised slightly, his hands smoothing back her hair, his eyes tender and gently amused. "Clementine Rose?"

She lifted her hips, drawing him deeper, into the dark center of where she wanted to warm Evan until he gave her everything. "Don't you tease me, Evan," she warned huskily and attempted a teasing smile. "Or I'll make you pay."

His slow boyish grin caught her, held her until joy bubbled out of her and she grinned back. She smoothed his damp chest, felt the racing heartbeat and knew it was for her and what would pass between them. His grin widened rakishly and he bent to nuzzle her breasts. "Then I guess you'll have to make me pay, Clementine Rose. Because you are truly the sweetest, lovingest woman that I have ever—''

She wiggled her hips and hugged him against her, pleased with the way he sank deeply into her. Because if ever there was a man who wasn't going to escape her at the height of her need, it was Evan Tanner.

She was certain he could withstand the heat and the passion storming through her. She felt that however strong she was, however needing, Evan's desire for her now would keep her safe.

"You are going to give me everything," she whispered, then bit his ear gently.

"Is that right, Clementine Rose?" he asked unevenly, his flushed face nuzzling the tender skin of her throat. Then he kissed her, and eased his fullness to the very deepest part of her being and she cried out his name as the circling passion tightened within her.

Evan closed his eyes and when he opened them, they burned her to her soul. "Everything," she demanded, even as Evan's body thrust deeply into hers.

They lifted high, flying against each other, claiming what each wanted and giving in to the desire feeding them. Above her, Evan's large body tightened just as she soared to the highest fire and exploded into shimmering sunlit pieces. She cried out her joy, savoring the rippling pleasure as Evan gave her everything.

When she came back to herself, Evan's head was resting on her breasts, his hands caressing her limp, warm body. "You are a greedy woman, Clementine Rose," he whispered shakily, one big hand gently gripping her bottom.

She swallowed uncertainly; her hands stopped stroking the taut, rippling muscles of his back.

She loved his back. She loved his chest—

She wiggled her still-aching breasts and found them instantly captured by his lips and worried by gentle bites. Evan suckled strongly and a second, gentler round of sensual tightening drew her against him.

She cleared her throat, unused to the loving play. "That will teach you," she managed to say.

He lifted to grin down at her.

Evan Tanner's grin was the most beautiful thing she had ever seen. "Sure will, Clementine Rose," he said in a tone rich with pleasure. "Can't say that I've ever been roped and bulldogged like that in my life."

Then he chuckled, his body gently bumping hers in all the right places.

She grinned back. Happiness on Evan Tanner was like sun on a tropical island, on a peach ripe and tasty, on a... Then Evan's smile softened and he bent to kiss her with the sweetest, gentlest piece of heaven she had ever tasted.

With him still lodged in her body, Clementine had fleeting images of little boys with Evan's wicked, wicked grin—of baby girls with the Tanners' gleaming raven hair. She turned the thought while smoothing his hair, keeping him close to her for a time.

His warm look down at her lingered, then he rubbed her arm briskly, his fingers clenching slightly as though he regretted the coming parting. "You're getting cold."

When he would have drawn away, Clementine speared her hands through his hair and tugged him down to her. She kissed him because she didn't want to frighten him too badly. Then she said, "Evan, if you say anything to ruin this, I will not be amused."

"Nothing is going to ruin this, Clementine Rose," he said firmly after a pause and kissed her again.

"Lie here with me.... Keep me warm," she whispered against his mouth.

He shuddered, then looked down at her breasts as if he'd never seen anything more beautiful. He shook his head, his eyes widening slightly as he fingered the torn lace of her bra. "Clementine, I didn't even take off my pants."

He sounded so outraged, so stunned, that she giggled and wrestled him beneath her. Evan lay there, his shirt open, scowling up at her darkly.

She was so glad he'd forgotten his sexual problem.

Really glad. In fact, she heard herself laugh outright with joy.

"Men don't take their ladies on the floor of dusty shacks, Clementine," he stated ominously as she slid into her sweater and tugged it down to her waist.

She arched an eyebrow and stroked his glorious chest with both open hands. She studied the motion of her pale fingers spearing through the dark hair and Evan clasped her wrists. "You're looking cocky for a lady who isn't used to—"

A dark flush ran up his throat and tinted his cheeks. "We'd better get dressed . . . I can't think with you looking like that."

She beamed. Happy little zings swirled inside her as she allowed him to dress her, all the time muttering about tearing bras and panties and yahoos who didn't take off their boots or pants.

His hand clenched her thigh when he knelt to tug on her boots, mumbling about red boots and red-hot women, which made her ego soar even more. He looked up at her grin and stated baldly, "I haven't had a woman in a long time. Haven't wanted one."

"Until today," Clementine returned happily, patting his head.

The more Evan muttered, the happier Clementine got. His passionate response to her wiped away every insecurity James and Morris and the tests had endowed upon her psyche. He pleased her right down to the curl of her toes in her boots. Evan scowled and grumbled, but allowed her to bend his head and pluck away the cobwebs from his hair and brush away the dust from his clothing. His hot stare at her unbound breasts under the sweater caused her to bounce just a little bit more as she walked around the old shack inspecting the shadows.

As if in a daze, Evan watched her, his eyes frequently jerking back to the spot on the floor where they had just made love.

Then he stood in the center of the small cold cabin and looked slowly around the shadows. She studied him carefully; something had eased in him, a distance growing between him and the cold past. He didn't resist when she took his hand and held it with both of hers. "Let's go," she said gently, lifting up on tiptoe to kiss his cheek.

He nodded curtly and minutes later, they rode silently back toward the ranch.

Evan reined Yuma to stop near a creek running through a stand of quaking aspens. He turned to look at Clementine, his expression stark with desire before he grimly dismounted and walked to stand beside Belle. Clementine slid into his arms, clinging to him as he carried her to the stream and gently placed her on her feet. His trembling hand traced her cheek, then he lifted her chin and kissed her gently.

"Do you hurt?" he asked in a deep, raw tone against her ear.

"A bit," she answered truthfully, startled by the flaring need to make love to him once more. She closed her eyes, willing away the fierce desire, because Evan might be shocked with a second dose of her loving. He'd made such strides against his problem.

Evan nuzzled her throat and rocked her in his arms. "Clementine Rose, you are quite the lady."

She stroked his taut neck, loving his familiar scent and the new ones that still clung to them. Evan shuddered and Clementine gripped his shoulders tighter, afraid that she would lose the intimacy they had gained. She refused to give way to his shadows, not just yet. "You could do that thing with your leg, Evan . . . you know—"

His lips curved slowly against her throat and his leg slid between hers, nudging her gently. "This?"

"Mmm."

He let out a hungry deep sound, then lifted her sweater and looked down at her breasts, cupping them in his large hands, studying the shape and weight. She cried out softly when his thumbs slid across the taut buds. Then Evan was jerking her to him, wrapping his arms around her tightly as though he were holding on to a lifeline in a torrent of whirling emotions. He shuddered, breathing unevenly against her throat.

"I hated him, Clementine. Hated my father as he lay dying." The admission ripped out of him in all its pain, the wound from long ago still raw. "He hated the world— your father, Jack, for holding the land when he couldn't. He blamed everybody."

Clementine stroked his back, aching for him. "You took care of him, Evan. You really didn't hate him. You were just a boy faced with a dark situation that you couldn't control."

"Right." The answer was flat. He held her, rocking her as the new aspen leaves shimmered above them and the spring rain began to fall.

Seven

Five days later, Evan knew that Clementine was worried about the trauma she may have inflicted on him the day they made love—he read it in every sad and guilty expression. He read it in the way she scanned her magazine quizzes, frowned thoughtfully at him, slashed new check marks and studied the results. She twisted her hands when he came too near, then suddenly rushed off to do something she'd forgotten.

Cookie had been waiting for them on the hotel's steps when they'd returned from the cabin. With their intimacy lying so new between them, Evan had not handled the situation well.

Dressed in her mining clothes and bragging about the strike she'd just tapped before coming to the hotel, Cookie's six-foot, well-padded frame and cheery brassy voice couldn't be ignored. Nor could her mule, who enraged Mosey to kick out a section of the barn boards again.

Clementine had leaned slightly against Evan and he had tensed, fighting his instincts to snare her close to him. The reaction was from years of seasoning, hiding his emotions. He hadn't had a sweetheart, and now, he'd felt as though he were sixteen and turning up on her parents' doorstep after making love. Then Clementine had blushed furiously and hurriedly excused herself to change clothes. Cookie had managed an ongoing conversation, answering her own questions while Evan stared at the closed door of the upstairs room. He helped Cookie move into the room Clementine had prepared, though he'd had other plans for the evening. They didn't include settling for a warmed apple dumpling, either.

His plan had been to love Clementine Rose until he was warmed clear through. To listen to those soft, little hungry purrs until the empty night slid away.

With Cookie's loud snores tearing through the hotel, Evan had spent sleepless nights thinking of the old bed creaking with Clementine's warm, soft body. He wanted to talk to her, to say the right things, in the right way... but his life hadn't prepared him with a list of speeches to pull out on demand and he didn't want to ruin the golden moments that had passed between them. For hours, Evan had mulled over sweet-talking scenes from movies. He thought about picking bouquets and presenting them to Clementine with just the right words.

Words weren't easy for a man who had kept his life locked inside him.

He'd relived the fiery passion and the joy, which still stunned him. Buried in Clementine's welcoming body, he'd known an intoxicating happiness that he hadn't believed existed.

He'd known then, just as he'd joined with her, why men made love to women—to give them children and to care and to protect them. There were selfish reasons a man made love—like snatching a bit of heaven for himself, a gentle soothing from the cold of life's scars. He'd reveled in the luxury of her breasts, the awesome wonder that they had been fashioned for him—for his touch.

To nourish babies.

Now Evan's mouth tightened as he looked at the twenty horses Mark had herded from the White ranch. Left to roam since last fall, they needed handling and calming before the guests arrived; accidents and lawsuits weren't on the company menu.

Evan's personal menu didn't include Clementine Rose as another man's hors d'oeuvre.

He had never claimed another woman with that dark, desperate fire, with that instinctive knowledge that he could be making a son. There had been protection, he'd seen to that. But the stark, natural urge was there—to make his child with Clementine Rose.

Evan jerked the leather thongs of his chaps tight around his thigh and tied the knot. He wasn't used to the jealousy that snared him when he thought of Clementine's ex-husband. Or the excuse of a man who had jilted her at the altar and devastated her. Evan wanted to catch that little jerk in some dark alley— The horses milled in the pen beside the corral where Mark stood holding the reins of a big, saddled gelding. "Ride 'em, cowboy," he said, grinning at Evan.

Evan grimly stepped up on the corral board and swung his leg over the top. He was too old to be so hot and bothered about a woman and to mope like a lovesick boy.

He tightened his leather gloves on the top board. For years, he'd had a good grip, a balance on his life—and the only dream he had left was to stand on Tanner land and if he were really lucky, the ranch for troubled boys would become reality. Lovemaking and babies and Clementine Rose were commodities he didn't understand and he shoved them back; he had a date with a wild-eyed gelding, not with the sympathy he'd begun to suspect Clementine Rose felt for him.

He'd had a taste of pity and wouldn't have it from a woman he'd wanted desperately enough to take on the dusty floor of the cabin. Evan scowled at the gelding. Clementine didn't have experience. Not a bit.... She'd moved against him tentatively; she deserved roses and violins and satin sheets—and he'd taken her on a dirty floor.

He paused in swinging his body over the fence, watching Clementine hurl from the porch. She crossed the sunlit ranch yard to grab his supporting leg. She hugged it against her body, leaving Evan to uncomfortably straddle the top corral board and his thoughts, which had stopped. "Don't, Evan. Oh, please don't. You've been injured enough. Oh, I am so sorry."

Her eyes begged him, tears streaming down her cheeks.

For a moment, Evan fell into the dark blue shimmering depths of her eyes—

"What's going on?" Mark asked warily as Clementine began to tug Evan's leg, which she had wrapped closely to her chest, attempting to pull him from the fence.

Evan tried to dislodge her gently while keeping his balance, his gloved hands locked to the boards. "Let go, Clementine," he ordered between his teeth and noted Cookie grinning hugely behind Clementine. "What are you grinning at?" he demanded rawly.

Clementine reached up to grip his belt with both hands, pulling at him with all her might. Evan balanced on the top board and distantly noted that bits of dough clung to her fingers. "You'll get hurt, Evan. I couldn't bear it...."

Evan tried for balance and failed; he fell toward Clementine, terrified that he would hurt her as they tumbled to the hard ground. With a quick jerk of his body, he took the brunt of the fall and Clementine landed on top of him. While he was catching his breath, she scrambled to sit on him and pinned his wrists above his head. The odd, sticky-moist lumps on her fingers stuck to his skin. "You're not riding those horses, Evan. I forbid you," she said fiercely.

Cookie stopped grinning and bent to swipe away Clementine's tears and pinched her nose with a handkerchief. "Blow."

Clementine obeyed, then said in a very prim ladylike tone, "Thank you, Cookie. I needed that."

Mark's roaring laughter startled the gelding who began bucking and kicking. A second later, Mark's six-foot-six, three-hundred-pound body scrambled over the corral fence, escaping the horse. He grinned at Clementine, who still straddled Evan. "Hi, Clementine."

"Mark, you will not let Evan hurt himself," she ordered fiercely.

"Hey, don't blame me," Mark retorted. "Evan grew up breaking horses."

She scowled up at him. "Well, he's done with that now. He can get hurt."

Evan dealt with the novelty of a gentle-natured woman who weighed almost eighty pounds less than him, facing Mark in a showdown to protect him. No one had protected him since he was a child.

"Get off me, Clementine," Evan muttered darkly while Mark crouched beside them, his head pivoted back and forth as he watched their warring expressions.

"This macho statement isn't necessary, Evan. Think of your injuries," she insisted as he lifted her from him and surged to his feet. He bent to pick up his hat and dusted it briskly against his chaps. He wasn't comfortable with anyone insisting on his safety and Clementine was acting like a hen with one chick.

Clementine rubbed the palms of her floury hands together and looked up at him, her eyes dark with concern. Her expression reminded Evan of her theory of his injuries. With Clementine's soft, warm thighs straddling him, he'd reacted instantly and knew that his functioning abilities were just fine. She stood there looking sweet and worried for him and Evan knew that he didn't want a heartbeat of her pity. He wanted more. He jammed his hat over his head, then placed his hand over Mark's wide grin and shoved slightly.

"Let it all out," Cookie encouraged, placing her hands on her ample hips. "You've been festering over something since I got here. You've been acting snarly, like somebody's taken something away from you. This little girl here is trying her best. She's not taking the ranch away from you. She's working to make it better."

"Oh, yes, Evan. Don't just grind your teeth and look all smoldery—express yourself. It's much better to let it all out. I can take it," Clementine urged earnestly. Mark's broad shoulders begin to shudder as he tried to contain his snickers.

"You want to know how I feel?" Evan lashed out at Clementine. "I'll tell you. I feel like riding every one of those broomtails into the dust and then going on a rip-roaring toot."

"Oh." She mulled that over a moment, then said firmly, "You're just transferring your anxieties about your... your illness."

"Illness?" Mark and Cookie asked sharply at the same time, their eyes searching him from head to foot.

Evan inhaled sharply. He knew what he needed and he didn't want Cookie and Mark for company, checking him out for illnesses, while he explained it to Clementine. Heathcliff began stomping at Clementine and Evan understood his irritation. "I'm riding those horses, Clementine," he said very evenly.

Her eyebrow lifted and quivered. "You do and I'll—"

"What?"

"Well...I don't know, but I'll think of something," she said boldly before marching off into the hotel.

Evan watched the fast sway of her hips beneath the tight jeans and shook his head. Clementine could frighten him down to his boots.

He rode every horse as though the very devil—or was it fear?—pursued him.

While he was occupied with the determination not to think about Clementine changing his life, Mosey ventilated the barn again.

Mark's mouth twitched and his eyes sparkled as he handed Evan a note that Cookie had given him. Evan wiped the sweat from his face with his forearm, then read Clementine's even, loopy handwriting.

I will not watch you injure yourself further. Also, I am truly sorry that I have injured you more and that you're still upset about Claudia. Be back in a few days. Cookie is showing me how to pan for gold and cook on a campfire. Zip, Slide, Mosey and Pow-Wow are with me. Please put the bread in the oven when it has raised enough. Three-seventy-five degrees for forty minutes. Please water Jethro and Sissie. One drop of their vitamins in a quart of room-temperature water.

Clementine.

Evan crushed the note in his leather gloves and while he was debating going after Clementine, baking bread, vitaminizing plants and his next move, Mark grinned widely.

"Oh, Evan, dear—you've got flour dough on your chaps and your belt," Mark sing-songed in a high voice between snickers.

"You know where she's at. Cookie always goes to the same place . . . by the old Chinese mine. You could go after her," Mark suggested on Friday, two days after the women, the mules and the greyhounds left to pan for gold. He pushed aside the crumbled crossword puzzle Evan had discarded, then picked up one of Jethro's limp vines and let it fall. He touched Sissie's broad drooping leaves and shook his head. "These plants have had it."

Evan stopped working on the accounts in the computer. He clicked the machine off when he realized that he had been staring at it and reanswering the questions to a quiz he'd just taken. Clementine had left the file of quizzes in an obvious, noticeable place. The "Profile of a Lover" test with Claudia's and Clementine's check marks had nettled him. He hadn't spent time considering techniques on the finer points of courting and making love to women; the question concerning time spent on foreplay had stunned him. The desperation he'd felt for Clementine had eliminated the tender, lingering pursuit described in the question.

Evan mulled the bright May day outside the window and realized that his hand had curled around the tutu-covered, rounded backside of the nearest bookend. He uncurled his fingers slowly.

Without Clementine, the old hotel was empty, a cold deadly shell, like the past.

Evan didn't know how to handle his current, unsettling emotions. More disturbing was the fact that he just wanted one of Clementine's hugs or kisses.

He pushed away the new crossword puzzle he'd tried working with little success. He wanted to hold Clementine in his arms and research foreplay.

He wanted better test scores.

He'd never been afraid to look at a bed... But Clementine's bed was another matter—he avoided glancing at it and his thoughts went flying back to a drowsy, feminine sigh—"Buddy-Bear..."

He'd never needed another person, not since he was a gangling teenager trying not to cry over his father's charity grave. Now the old hotel echoed with scents that reminded him of Clementine—

Evan stood up, glared at Mark and walked out of the room.

Mark followed him to the kitchen and poked the black crusts of the four loaves of bread on the table and shook his head. "Boy... you have purely flunked bread baking."

Evan leveled Mark a dark you-know-where-you-can-take-it look. A good friend, Mark blandly returned the look. "I've been there," he said finally. "Tell you what, Evan. My wife is in Wenatchee this weekend, staying with her mother, and I've got tractor parts to pick up in Okanogan. When's the last time you got out of here? What about heading out for Okanogan, checking out that Appaloosa stud I'm thinking of buying and having a beer with me?"

Then he picked up a pump mist bottle, filled it with water and began squirting the new plant starts on the windowsill. He met Evan's questioning look with a lonesome, wistful expression and a shrug. "My wife—old S.J.—likes plants. A guy starts liking stuff like spritzing plants when his wife is gone overnight."

Evan wondered what he could do to get back in Clementine's good graces. Plant vitaminizing and spritzing might not fill the bill.

Lying on a cot, Evan watched a spider cross the jail's ceiling and considered the tavern's good-natured brawl between old friends. He'd been in a few and knew the difference between sheer meanness and letting off steam.

Fred Weaver should have never compared good sex to ruffled, gingham curtains in the same breath. The obscure remark had to do with comparing sexual foreplay to ruffled curtains, a "pretty" covering to the real thing—and something that women liked.

After Fred's sage insight, some cowboy had been affronted when his girlfriend had asked Evan to dance. He had just stared at her, thinking about Clementine and how sweetly she fit his arms. Believing she had been insulted, the woman had slapped him.

Mark had excused himself from the brewing set-to because "old S.J." didn't like his six-foot-six, three-hundred-pound body bruised or abused. She'd once tracked down a man who had hit Mark and she had called him out; the bucket over his head had required another man to yank it off. The two brothers of the man who thought his girlfriend had been insulted had been Evan's rodeo competitors and decided to even the score—the three brothers against Evan. Since Evan was in the mood to brawl—an event he hadn't entertained for years—he obliged.

The jailhouse spider began spinning a web in a corner and Evan sorted through his thoughts as he watched—it seemed an appropriate thing to do at five o'clock on a Saturday morning. Clementine was like that, Evan decided—busily tangling him in gossamer, fragile emotions that unsettled the hell out of him. The brawl had seemed safer.

The spider began to lower itself just as the jailer's key turned in the main door and Clementine followed the deputy into the room filled with cells. "He's mine," she said frostily as Evan rose slowly to his feet. "Can I take him home now?"

Minutes later, Evan jammed his personal effects into his pockets, while Clementine watched. He jerked away from her tentative finger along his cheek, and resisted a minute before she tugged him down to kiss his eye. She turned to the deputy. Her eyebrow lifted and quivered. "Evan has a black eye," she stated in a tight, ominous voice.

"Yes, ma'am. He was in a fight," the deputy answered around his toothpick and his grin. "Public disturbance. Just tucked 'em in here for safekeeping and to let them finish their cowboy songs in peace. They had a real good quartet going. The rest of the men have already been collected by their women."

"I have been gold panning or I would have been here sooner," Clementine said righteously. Then she leaned toward him, her hands on the table. "I can assure you that it wasn't his fault. Evan is a gentle man." When the deputy moved his toothpick to the other corner of his grin, Clementine placed her arm through Evan's. "Come along, Evan."

He felt the dull red shade rising up the back of his neck as she waited.

He refused to look at the grinning deputy, or to comment on the way Clementine ground the gears in Mark's stock-hauling pickup.

"Are you hurt, Evan?" Clementine demanded, screeching second gear into third as they barreled down Highway 97.

"I'm just dandy," he answered grittily and sank into the seat of the truck. He pulled his hat over his eyes and tried to sleep; he hadn't had much of it in the jail. The cot had creaked, reminding him of Clementine on the bed. He'd been missing Clementine too much and remembering how the cold tight knot that had ridden him most of his life had unfurled while they made love.

Clementine interrupted his bid for peace with a prim, tight sentence. "If it will make you feel better, you can hang that dreadful Miss Matilda Dryer picture . . . at least until the guests arrive. I don't want them shocked."

Evan thought about the male guests toasting Miss Matilda and bygone days of "real women." The nightlong, final barbecue, beer-drinking, belching, range-song-singing poker party was the perfect windup to a western vacation. Clementine's hippopotamuses and ruffled gingham curtains would fit in just fine.

Clementine didn't know why Evan insisted that Brent—instead of herself—drive the truck loaded with her antique furniture on the back roads and across the fields to the hotel. Evan and the movers had packed the contents of the shipping van into the truck and on the backs of the horses, which Brent had waiting for them in Loomis.

The baby chicks, which had been delivered that morning, cheeped in the cardboard box tied to the horse behind Evan's. Periodically, he leveled a glare at the box, then at her. She wondered why he was in such a dark mood, when she had been frantic with worry.

She didn't mention Jethro's and Sissie's poor condition or the burned bread, which had hardened to bricks in the pans.

She ached horribly for Evan, who was evidently still mourning his loss of Claudia. She ached for herself, because the tender, sweet way he'd made love to her hadn't seemed to matter.

She gripped her saddlehorn until her fingers hurt. Her heart tore apart as she wondered if Evan was thinking of how he should have made love to Claudia.

Clementine straightened her shoulders and lifted her chin. She wouldn't substitute for anyone. Evan Tanner had a thing or two to learn about lovemaking with her.

She decided to be very polite and businesslike around Evan. Just until her own emotions settled and she could get back to rescuing him.

Brent had picked up Mark and "old S.J." along the way, and the three men, Cookie and Clementine worked to unpack her possessions and several bolts of red gingham material. S.J., a perky blonde, loved the way Clementine had used the junkyard bottles and hardware to decorate the hotel. She loved the idea of gingham curtains and Clementine noted how Mark beamed at his wife, while treating her like a very prized lady.

Still in his dark mood, Evan had studied the bolts of gingham, then he had looked at the windows and then he was gone.

His expression was the bleakest Clementine had ever seen and she longed to place her arms around him. She wanted to hold him because he needed love and because she needed to know that he was safe. She needed Evan to hold her against him, to hear the thump-thump of his heart beneath her cheek and the solid feel of his arms holding her.

On her way to the chuck wagon and Evan the next day, Clementine passed the rooster, Heathcliff, who tilted his red comb, eyeing her. The noonday sun lay in iridescent shades on his dark red feathers as he jumped, stomping the dust in a threatening manner. She decided it was a territorial dispute, much like Evan's dislike of her encroaching on his idea. She continued on her way. She refused to be intimidated by either male.

"Evan, since I haven't been on a roundup, I need your input—" Clementine's fast stride to the chuck wagon stopped. She gripped the newsletter she had been working on—directed to clients and tourist magazines—and stared at Evan's bare, gleaming chest, which was just inches from her face.

"'Afternoon, Clementine," he said huskily as her eyes slowly lifted to his warm, amused ones, one of which was swollen and bruised.

She tried to think and found herself saying, "How's your eye?"

He grinned slowly, then tossed the hammer he had been using on the chuck wagon into it. His gaze ran down her blouse and jeans to her red boots, then back up to her face...where it lingered on her lips, which she licked. "Needs a kiss. One of yours, Clementine Rose. Are you going to kiss my eye or not?"

Clementine backed up a step, arching her head to look up at him.

Evan at play could take the breath from any woman. He reached to smooth her hair behind her ear. The tender gesture stunned her.

"Thank you for collecting me yesterday, Clementine," he said gently. While she tried to place this warm, teasing man with the one who had disappeared after unloading the horses and the truck, he asked, "Are you going to kiss my eye?"

She cleared her throat. She wanted to kiss his eye, his curving lips, his chest, his— "Well, I..."

Then Evan leaned down. She studied the blackened eye, gleaming at her. She kissed it and the small bruise along his jaw and the tiny shaving cut on his cheek.

He straightened slowly, tugged her hair and said, "Feels better already."

She bristled a bit. "I never should have told you my middle name. Claudia used to taunt me, calling me Tulip and Daffodil and Geranium. If you start that, you'll never see another apple dumpling."

Evan's swollen eye gleamed and his good one widened as his eyebrows lifted in an innocent expression. His hand lay on his chest as if taking a pledge. "Clementine Rose, I would never do that."

Then he grinned, bent to slide his hands under her bottom and lifted her. Off-balance, she reached to grip his shoulders and Evan urged her legs around his hips. "There, that's more like it," he murmured in a satisfied tone as he walked, carrying her to a shadowy nook of the barn, nuzzling and kissing her neck with every step. Then he eased down to an old crate and sat holding her, straddling him, as if the occurrence happened every day.

Clementine straightened her shoulders and unlatched her fingers from his dark, sun-warmed skin. Greedy for the feel of him, her rebellious hands almost refused to release him. Evan studied her carefully, then his fingers caressed her hot cheek. "Thank you, Clementine Rose, for rescuing me."

"You are very welcome. . . . You were upset about me claiming you," she returned uncertainly, stroking the hard muscle at the back of his neck. Evan needed stroking and care.

He arched against her hand, rolling his neck slightly and finding her palm again. She rubbed the taut cords while Evan considered her thoughtfully. "I haven't been claimed a lot in my life, Clementine Rose," he said rawly. "It takes a bit of getting used to."

"I'll protect you, Evan." Clementine laid her head on his shoulder and wrapped him tightly in her arms and legs, giving him her protection. Her father had told her of Evan's running away from foster homes and she wished she'd been there for him. She wished she'd been there when he fought the bandits in the oil fields and when he hurt his back in Nigeria.

His smile curved along her throat and his hands massaged her back, circling to rest beneath her breasts. "You were tough on the deputy."

Clementine's thoughts were focused on Evan's hands and their vicinity. She reached down, grabbed his wrists and jerked his hands higher until they opened over the aching softness of her. She cried out softly as he caressed her gently; his face heated instantly against her skin. "Sweet," he murmured unevenly as Clementine moved closer to the gentle, seeking kisses.

He lifted her hands to his face and kissed each palm, flicking the center with his tongue. He nibbled each finger as if tasting the cinnamon rolls she had just baked, his eyes darkening as they met hers. Then Evan wrapped an arm around her and held her close, his mouth slanting hungrily down on hers. She opened to him, giving him what he demanded, and taking what she needed.

"Let me see you," he said rawly, his hand pressing against her breast. His fingers slid to the first button of her blouse as his eyes held hers, then the second... When her breasts lay bare to him, Evan lowered his head to slowly suckle and taste, to cherish her gently.

She began to hum—she needed the distraction to stop herself from pushing Evan back to the hay and kissing him and loving him.

"What are you doing, Clementine?" he asked with a smile in his voice.

"Oh, nothing," she answered in a high, tight tone as her body began to contract and melt, then tighten again. She wanted him locked in her, a part of her body, the fires heating and the storms brewing—

He placed his cheek against hers, the roughness chafing slightly as he nuzzled her and his hands caressed her breasts, which ached for the warmth of his mouth. "You know what I'm thinking about?"

"No..." Clementine was deep in her own thoughts. She placed her hands over his chest, loving the rippling muscles beneath her palms. She speared her fingers through the wonderful mat of hair and wistfully traced the line running down into his waistband.

Evan placed his hand over hers as she started to unbuckle his belt. "Clementine Rose, the next time we make love, we're doing it proper," he promised darkly.

She shook her head. "It was...very...nice, Evan. I mean it was very proper. Wasn't it?" A horrifying thought went through her and she looked at him. "Evan, did I do something wrong? Have I damaged you that badly?"

"I'd say you did everything just right," he said tenderly.

"I've frightened you, haven't I?" she continued worriedly. "I know I acted selfishly, taking what I wanted—"

Evan sat very still. "What are you saying, Clementine?"

She cleared her throat and looked away to Heathcliff who was continuing his sideways stomp-dance toward them. She hoped the shadows would hide her blush. "When I ravished you in that cabin, Evan," she said very precisely, "I'm afraid that I wanted you very much."

"Yes . . . ?" he prompted slowly, kissing one corner of her mouth, then the other.

"I wanted you desperately," she corrected, deciding to bare her deepest heart to him. "You made me feel very desirable, and that isn't something a person like me extracts from a man very often. I'm afraid it is I who must thank you."

"Clementine Rose...you are one desirable lady," Evan murmured unsteadily as she wiggled more comfortably on his lap and his hand found and tightened over her breast.

"In another minute, Evan, I'm afraid that—"

His lips nibbled at hers, soothing, enchanting, wooing.

Clementine tried to restrain herself and lost. She wrapped both arms around his neck and kissed him with the hungry depths of her soul.

Evan didn't seem to mind as he bore her down to the haystack and spread himself over her as if he were coming home. Taking her hands in his, he kissed each one, then placed them on his chest. "I like that," he said simply as her fingers began fluttering over him.

She cherished his weight and safety, arching against him. She tangled her legs with his, keeping him close when he would have braced his body away.

* * *

When she returned to the computer, she realized that she hadn't gotten his opinion of the newsletter article she was writing.

At dusk, Evan carried the old treadle machine into the saloon and placed it near a window. He wiped a rag over it, nodded at Cookie and Clementine as though he carried in antique sewing machines every day, and said, "Sewing machine. Use it."

He started to walk out, stopped, then turned to Clementine whose eyes had begun to fill with tears. She realized what the machine meant to him and he was offering it to her.

His eyebrows jerked together and the tiny vein beat in his temple. "It's old...you'll want to order an electric one," he began in a raw tone then stopped as Clementine hurled herself into his arms and clung to him. For the second time that day, Evan lifted her legs around him. He glanced at Cookie, then kissed Clementine gently. He nuzzled her throat, whispered comforting words and walked out of the hotel bearing her with him.

Eight

"I don't want Clementine or Cookie to worry. Whoever is causing trouble is getting to be a real pest—he's ordered a bunch of fancy doodads in my name. Like a video on how to rumba and a hummingbird spout for a garden hose. Whoever is doing it is just letting me know he's around. This morning, Mack Smith's llama was with the cattle in the north pasture. Mack wasn't happy that Buford had escaped, which I don't think he did. Buford is too lazy to go too far. Someone helped him.... You're keeping this between us, aren't you?" Evan asked Brent as they stood in the ranch yard. He handed Brent the rope he had been swirling around his boots.

"Sure am. I'll watch for that missing saddle, Evan. You say the horn has tooled leather?" Brent answered as he twirled the lasso as Evan had just showed him. The teenager flung the loop at a post and when it circled the wood, he jerked the rope tight.

Evan placed his hand on Brent's shoulder and nodded approvingly at his victorious grin. "Good job, son."

Brent flipped the rope from the post. "You like kids, don't you? Why didn't you ever have any?"

Evan studied the borrowed herd grazing in the late May sun, the calves frisking in the meadow. The thought had been on his mind since he'd made love to Clementine Rose; he'd mulled it over slowly and decided that he'd missed having children. The boys he hoped to help would fill a portion of that emptiness. He answered Brent's question as carefully as he could. "Time just went by. I thought a lot about it when I was younger. I wanted Tanner blood holding Tanner land so a part of me would go on. Making a baby is important. The why and the wants need careful thought. A child is a responsibility, a gift and just about the best, most important accomplishment of a man's life—if he wants to be a father. Some men don't want children and if they make that decision, they're being responsible, too. Children are a commitment.... It's the same if a man adopts. But anyway—planned or not—when a man is lucky enough to have children, he'd better take care of them."

"My dad doesn't want me around." The teenager shifted restlessly. "You're saying that when Mary and I get—worked up, that I'd better do some serious thinking, right?"

"Uh-huh. See what's inside yourself and know who you are and what you want, Brent. You're someone pretty important and who you choose to marry will be someone special, too. She might just drop into your life when you least expect it." Like Clementine, Evan thought.

"Mary makes me hot," Brent muttered. "It's hard to think, you know? Her folks are fighting all the time and she thinks we should run away and get married. You know...make our own family.''

"Some people start that way and it works out. But you think long and hard about that, okay?''

While Brent swirled the rope and turned his thoughts, Evan was remembering marrying for the wrong reasons. Though his pain was long ago, Evan doubted he would ever marry for love. While he cared for Clementine, respected her and cherished her and hungered for her, he feared love. He didn't know if he could love, the deepdown true kind that songs on the radio described.

Maybe Claudia had sensed that he couldn't give her that part of himself. At first, he'd been hurt by her choice to marry another man. Now he wondered if she was right.

Clementine Rose deserved that from a man—*"I want everything,"* she'd said.

The sting of cold fear shot through him. He wanted the best for Clementine. The thought that she might go waltzing off with another man—a man who knew how to love—caused his heart to hurt.

"I wish Mom or Dad would talk to me like you do,'' Brent stated and flushed. "He just threw some protection at me and said to watch it and not to bother him. Not that Mary and I have done anything...yet.''

Evan placed his hand on the boy's thin shoulder. "Your dad is right. Protection is important. But when a man makes love to a woman, it's a responsibility, too. There should be some feeling in him for her, other than the want to get rid of an urge. Like he's coming home and like respect and friendship...or admiring the way she is...caring for her.... A good, sweet feeling about her and what's passing between them. She should have that same feeling about him.''

Did Clementine have that coming-home feeling when they had made love? "... *I want everything....*"

"Nothing lasts. Mom and Dad didn't even like each other."

"Sure, they did. Time just turned things around. They wouldn't have had you if they didn't. You're pretty special, Brent."

Brent squinted at the sunlight tangling in the garden's old grapevines, then at Clementine who was using the lure of a carrot to coax a young rabbit out of hiding. Evan watched her, thinking that she had more love in her than two women; she deserved just as much back. He envied the rabbit basking in her attention. Then Brent was saying, "How does it feel when you... well, with a woman, Evan? I mean, the stuff you were just talking about—feelings?"

Evan thought about how Clementine made him feel while they made love. The rabbit hopped from the brush and began nibbling on the carrot in Clementine's hand. Evan inhaled sharply, realizing she had drawn him from the shadows for just a time. He took the rope, started swirling it and made it circle his body. He twirled it behind him, hopped into the circle of it, then out and gave it back to Brent. "First of all, the feelings startle a man when he's not used to sharing what's in him. He's warm, real warm, and not just from sex, either. Like she fills a part of him that was missing. Like she's melted the cold away and replaced it with summer and flowers and fresh-baked apple dumplings with cinnamon. Like he wants to laugh out loud because he's happy he's alive and has found her. Everything that passed before, the hurting, doesn't matter—because everything else is just so much dust."

"Yeah." Brent looked away and frowned. "I never thought about it like that—that making love needs to matter before and later. I like being here. Clementine and you treat me like I . . . well, like I'm someone special . . . a friend. Thanks, Evan."

"Thanks for coming...and for helping keep an eye out for whoever is causing the problems."

"Yeah. Right. Glad to help," Brent muttered, then hurried to his horse. "Have to get back to our place. Dad wants me to make an appearance for some rich friends. He wants me to clean up and hang around a couple of hours, then get lost. See you."

Evan watched the boy run, then leap into his saddle. There was an uneasiness about Brent when discussing the mischief around the ranch. He needed attention just as Evan had as a troubled teenager.

Brent glowed when Clementine asked him to help her— to taste her cake batter and to plant her herb seedlings. He held the clothes basket for her when she hung out the wash— Evan smiled, remembering Clementine's reaction to the used washer that he'd reconditioned and installed. There was just something about a soft woman hurling herself at him and locking him in her arms and legs. The hundred or so kisses around his face didn't hurt, either.

Every time he sat and worked his crossword puzzles, trying to concentrate while Clementine used the old treadle machine, the cold pain in Evan eased and warmed. He found himself just looking at her sitting and sewing in the little corner sewing nook. While he missed Matilda— at times, lingering with her and listening to the romantic songs on the radio, Clementine had her own charm. Yards of red gingham spilled everywhere, reminding him of Fred Weaver's insight connecting gingham and windows and women.

Foreplay was definitely on his list for events with Clementine.

Evan glanced at the rabbit nibbling happily away at the carrot in Clementine's hand. She'd coaxed Evan into the loving feeling, if not love. *"I want everything...."*

Could he give her everything? Did he know how? Had he walked too long in shadows and fears, the scars lying thick around his heart? Would he hurt her, or were the shadows safer?

Clementine watched Brent ride away as Evan stood alone in the ranch yard, twirling the rope. She stood slowly so as not to frighten the rabbit, hopped over the row of green beans Brent had helped her plant, then the new bright green line of lettuce. She walked to Evan and he quickly coiled the rope into one hand. "You keep feeding that rabbit and you'll be missing that lettuce you're so proud of. He'll bring his friends to dinner," he said with a slow, almost shy, lopsided grin. "Or we could have rabbit stew."

"Not my little bunny." She wondered if she'd caught Evan thinking about Claudia or Miss Matilda Dryer, the clothesless hussy. Because Clementine didn't want to share him—her greed for Evan surprised her—she reached to draw him down for a kiss and noted with satisfaction that he didn't resist her tug. She leaned against him slightly, certain that he could withstand her weight—he'd been carrying her often enough lately. Of course there was little else he could do, when she leg-locked him.

Evan responded instantly to her leg-locks, she thought as his lips hovered and brushed hers. She nestled against him, reveling in the hard muscles beneath his clothing, the safe thump-thump of his heart beneath her cheek. Then because she was afraid that she would frighten him, Clementine forced herself away from him. Evan's dark gray gaze took in her face and strolled downward to caress her breasts.

"Clementine Rose, you are looking fine this morning," he drawled in a husky tone that curled her toes. It was the same tone he used when he'd carefully fitted his hands over her bare skin— She flushed, remembering how she had torn away her shirt and her bra last night, straddling Evan beneath her.

She flushed deeper, remembering him nuzzling her stomach and kissing her belly button. She'd squirmed and giggled and found the ticklish spot on his ribs and returned the favor. But when she'd kissed Evan's navel, he'd tensed and gripped her shoulders. "Stop...better stop that, Clementine Rose," he'd whispered urgently, a thread of fear running through his voice.

Then he'd drawn her down beside him and they'd lain there, snuggled together on the old quilt in the hayloft. Listening to the old barn and Evan's heartbeat, Clementine had loved the peaceful stillness. After a while, Evan had straightened her clothing and walked her to the hotel. He'd kissed her on the front porch with the tenderest kiss she'd ever tasted.

She wanted more. She wondered if there were tests to determine the reasons for Evan's restraint. She wondered if there was a quiz to determine why Evan didn't want his belly button kissed.

She thought of how she'd nuzzled his flat hard stomach, loving the pine and soap and male scent of him, the way his hands had speared into her hair and the way his breath had caught. He'd moved restlessly beneath the light tether of her hands and had groaned shakily. She'd never considered herself a sensuous woman and the knowledge that Evan—spread out like her private smorgasbord—reacted to her for whatever reason, delighted her.

She resolved to do plenty of kissing and belly-button nuzzling when it came to Evan Tanner. He'd given her joy in that moment when they made love and she wanted more. Lying in that old bed every night and thinking of its passionate history caused her to want to toss Evan on the creaking springs and—

"... I've been thinking," Evan was saying now as he watched the cattle graze, and began swirling the lasso around his boots. "Your idea for a computer electronic message center for the guests is good. We can take reservations that way and answer questions. Then the guests can use it for a fee, to leave messages. Since we're not always available for the telephone, the messages can wait until we draw them off the computer. We won't need extra equipment and we can check into the messages twice daily. You might want to add that in your newsletter."

"I will and you can teach Maud rope tricks, Evan."

"No." He flicked the rope and it leapt to circle a post. "Women might not be on our guest list, remember?"

Another flick took it from the post. "But we're considering it, aren't we?" Clementine asked ominously and felt her eyebrow quivering. She touched and stilled it. Only Evan could manage to anger her.

"Maybe. Maybe not." Then he grinned and her anger flew away into the sagebrush-covered mountains. "I bet you jumped rope when you were a little girl."

Clementine grinned up at him. "I could do double-rope red-hots faster than anyone."

"I'll just bet," he said in a slow, husky tone that caused her to shiver and that erased James's and Morris's damaging comments about her unexciting sexuality.

* * *

"These look good," Evan said, studying the hot cinnamon rolls Clementine held up to him the next day. He drew off his leather gloves, took the plate from her and placed it on the chuck-wagon floorboards beside him. "But this looks better."

Then he reached down, put his hands under her arms and lifted her up easily. Standing against him in the old chuck wagon, Clementine was kissed hungrily. When she was released, Evan grinned boyishly and she tried to line up her thoughts as she scrambled from the wagon. She tugged down her T-shirt and Evan's gaze slashed to the twin nubs pushing against the material. She crossed her arms in front of her. "You cannot just grab me like that, Evan Tanner, not when the guests are around. They'll be arriving tomorrow—the first of June. What will they think?"

He looked at her for a moment, then leapt from the wagon and walked into the barn, ignoring her.

Clementine hurried after him. She really didn't want to hurt him; he was responding so nicely. She snared his belt just as he reached the barn door nearest the pasture. "Evan, you're not thinking that they'll think you're making points—ah...making—that you kiss me because you want an advantage in the ranch business, do you?" she said as he kept walking, pulling her behind him.

"I'm not crazy about making love to a senior partner on the dirty floor of a cabin, Clementine Rose. Or the thought that you might be trying to make up for two other Barlow women jilting Tanner men. I don't need sympathy, insurance for whatever disabilities you think I have, and I sure as hell don't need rescuing. Let's get that clear right now," he said flatly between his teeth as he came to an abrupt halt. He looked at the cattle grazing in the sunshine. ''What do you think about her?''

''Cows? Her...what?'' she asked, terrified that Evan would say that making love had been a mistake. She gripped his belt tighter.

He grimly nodded to a small white cow mottled with brown spots. A calf nudged the cow's udder looking for her dinner. ''Her name is Daisy, Clementine Rose. You'll have to learn how to milk because she's giving too much for one calf. Her milk is rich, good for making butter.''

He took a deep breath and added, ''She belonged to the Monroes. They've got a Holstein herd now and Daisy won't take the electric milker. They were going to sell her at an auction. I thought she should stay put—here where she was born. Sam Monroe said Daisy's mother had her in the cottonwood stand close to the old cabin. The old cow fought off coyotes and kept Daisy alive until Sam arrived. Then the cow died. It seems like Daisy has the right to be here. The price was good.''

Clementine met Daisy's soft, liquidy brown eyes. Evan Tanner might bristle when he was petted, but he was a loving man. He didn't really care about getting Daisy as a bargain; he cared about *her*. Tears burned Clementine's eyes and her throat closed with emotion as she remembered how Evan cared for Cookie's arthritis, Brent's loneliness, and the assortment of unwanted animals.... Like Jasmine, the descented skunk who was no longer wanted as a household pet and had no way to protect herself in the wild. Few men would rise at two o'clock in the morning to repair the damage Mosey's hooves had done in the barn, then wrap the old mule's lower legs with rags to cover the warming liniment. ''Oh...Evan...''

He looked down at her warily and his broad shoulders tensed. ''You're not going to cry, are you?''

Tangled in her emotions, Clementine simply leaned against Evan. She tucked her face against his throat and wrapped her arms around him, breathing the familiar scent of him. "Clementine Rose," he whispered unevenly against her hair. Then his arms came slowly and securely around her, just the way she wanted.

The twenty men of all ages slid off their horses. Each man held a monogrammed bedroll in one hand and small, but expensive luggage in the other. They took in the hotel, the cattle in the field, Cookie standing on the front porch and Clementine.

She smiled at them, silently wishing that when it was time to go, each guest would return to his home without harm. Evan's dark gaze shot at her, then at the men, whom he instructed curtly that nobody else would unsaddle their horses—so they'd better do it themselves. Clementine watched, fascinated as Evan tipped back his dusty hat, locked his knees within the worn chaps and hooked his thumbs in his belt. "I'm the top ramrod of this outfit, boys, so what I say goes. If you want to drink, you're out of luck until we toast Miss Matilda Dryer at the last fandango. When the weather is wet, you'll sleep on the hotel floor. When it's not, you sleep outside under the stars—we charge you for the rattlers you try to sneak into your bedrolls. Grub is served at dawn, noon straight-up, and supper is when I say so. If you want a bath, there's the creek and a tub on Saturday night. Get to know your horse—he's yours for your stay."

Evan nodded to the porch. "That's Cookie and Clementine. Cookie knows more about this country than anyone and she can outyodel anyone I ever knew. Clementine is the boss. When she says fetch—you fetch. When she says carry—you do it. Anyone stepping out of line will have to answer to me." Then he nodded curtly, jerked his hat low and unsaddled Yuma. After opening the gate to the corral and shooing Yuma through, Evan stopped to watch the comedy of the greenhorns stirring up the ranch yard dust and shook his head.

Cookie, Evan and Clementine sat on the front porch, watching the men. Evan rested his hand on Clementine's knee and shook his head as one man tried to kiss and pet his horse into standing still. Perkins, the retired astronaut turned banker, wore his cherished "woolly" chaps and ten-gallon hat. He handled his horse methodically and began swaggering to the barn with his saddle. His chaps frightened Lamont's horse, and the French restaurateur let out a stream of fluid Bronx-accented threats. Evan's thumb caressed the softness of Clementine's inner knee. His long fingers tightened and he looked down at the soft flesh beneath his hand. "Clementine, you are wearing shorts," he muttered indignantly.

"Yes?" she returned in a slow, questioning tone, encouraging him to go on.

"Evan," Cookie warned curtly.

He frowned at the older woman over Clementine's head. "They'll see her legs."

Clementine stretched out her legs in front of her, studying them and wondering what it was the men would see. Then a psychiatrist's playboy son dropped his saddle to the ground and smiled at her.

Evan shot the playboy a dark look. "Look at that. He's got fangs. Clementine's legs are long and buck-naked," Evan stated baldly to Cookie who was grinning.

"She's wearing her red boots," Cookie retorted easily. "They cover most of her legs."

"You don't know what red boots can do to a man. Two weeks of looking at those legs and red boots and we'll have real problems," Evan returned darkly, his fingers gently tightening on Clementine's knee. His thumb eased to the tender back of her knee and stroked it lightly. The vein in his temple throbbed slowly as if he were concentrating on a matter of deep importance.

Clementine closed her eyes and found herself wondering about working her way down from Evan's belly button to kiss the back of his knee. Because he seemed so upset, Clementine leaned slightly closer to Evan.

"Don't you hug me," he said unsteadily and stood abruptly. He snared the bridle of the rearing horse nearest him and scowled at the financial advisor. In seconds, Evan had uncinched the saddle and tossed it at the would-be cowboy. "Tack room is in the barn. Put it on the board with a number matching the saddle. That's your number from now on, got it?"

Clementine smiled back at the young man watching her from the yard. "Evan must be tired. He's not very hospitable to the guests."

"My, my, my," Cookie said, and began to blow the bubble gum Evan had brought her from town. The bubble popped on her face. "He's upset."

Evan remained upset and moody for the next two weeks. He was especially dark-tempered when Clementine sat down at the evening campfire and opened her file of quizzes. The men lay on their bedrolls, trying to ignore Wilkins who was determined to learn how to play the harmonica. Evan left abruptly when Clementine began the "Profile of a Lover" quiz.

The "drovers" and "cowhands" practiced keeping on their horses, going in one direction, and moving the cattle from pasture to pasture. They got better at swaggering, telling tall tales, playing poker and chopping wood.

When not cooking and telling old-timer tales, Cookie made eyes at a New York publisher who also loved bubble gum; they huddled over ideas for her first pioneer no-lard cookbook.

On the cattle drive, which lasted four days, Evan insisted that Clementine and Cookie ride on and stay near the chuck wagon. He was very precise about where the men and the women should lay in the chuck wagon, then he slept exactly between them. Zip and Slide ran after jackrabbits, quail and sage hens. They stirred up skunks, as well, then sheepishly rode in the chuck wagon. The night of the roast rattlesnake or wieners-and-beans dinner, Evan played a soulful harmonica, the lonesome music drifting up on the smoke to the night sky. The music was old, coming from campfires long ago when the cattle lowed in the moonlight and lonely men ached for the warmth of women and children. He'd gotten the skill and the songs from his father. According to Jack Barlow, Ben Tanner's harmonica could make hardened criminals cry; Evan's music curled around her and she sniffed just once while Cookie sobbed loudly.

The magic ended when seven guests drew out their new harmonicas and Evan tutored them.

Then he had looked across the campfire to Clementine and her heart stilled—the loneliness and longing in Evan's expression caused her to take a step toward him. Then she realized that he would reject her hugs and kisses in front of the men, so instead she blew him a kiss.

Though he didn't move from his bedroll and saddle, lightning crackled and heat rose in the quiet still air between them as Evan stared at her. She sensed that in another minute he would surge from the ground, walk to her and carry her off into the night.

Instead, the coyotes howled, the greyhounds whined and Cookie muttered, "Fatback, beans and pay dirt" in her sleep.

Clementine lay in her chuck wagon bedroll listening to Cookie snore and to Evan's music. She petted Zip's and Slide's smooth heads, which lay across her stomach, and ached to hold Evan tight and cuddle him. If left alone, he could return to mulling over the Barlow-Tanner feud and Claudia's jilting and sink into a fit of sexual dysfunction. Clementine straightened out her toes in the bedroll, stretching just as far and tight as she could. Evan's lovemaking had been perfect.

She hoped he didn't lose the progress he had been making—the dark, riveting, hungry looks that stopped her thoughts, heated her body and made her think of nuzzling his belly button.

While Evan didn't appreciate her help with crossword puzzles, she wouldn't allow him to wade through the past ill fortunes of the Tanners—the jilting of Roy by Elise Barlow, and the Tanner-Barlow brawls and the time Lonny Barlow released his pet buffalo bull into the Tanners' cow pasture.

When the cattle drive was almost ended, Clementine found Evan looking up the rocky incline toward the old cabin. He sat on Yuma, looking like a cowboy from a century ago, and stroked his cheek with his missing thumb.

Then he turned to her, deliberately seeking her out on the chuck wagon. Their eyes held and fire leapt on the sunshine between them, warming her in her deepest, most feminine essence.

Evan Tanner wanted her more than he wanted to linger in his painful memories.

Because she wanted him just as desperately, she caught him while he was cooling off—pouring a dipper of water over his head—and pushed him back against the chuck wagon, out of sight of the men.

"What . . . ?" he began as she snared his neck with her arms, arched against him and kissed him until he was warm and trembling and hungry.

"Take that, Evan Tanner," she whispered shakily as his gloved hands reached down to cup and caress her bottom.

"Oh, I intend to, Clementine Rose," he whispered back and urged her against his thighs. He was very sweet and arousable, she decided as Evan deepened the kiss, slanting his mouth over hers and tantalizing her until she suckled his tongue.

Cookie's and the men's distant yodeling slid between them and Evan reluctantly put Clementine away from him. "She's just about as welcome as poison ivy," he muttered darkly and looked so frustrated that Clementine began to smile.

He grinned back at her.

Clementine ignored the last fandango party downstairs and the lurid toasts to Matilda, the hussy. She added expenses, inventoried "grub supplies," collected all the electronic mail and sent back late confirmations to the guests applying for a two-week session in August. She gave Cookie lessons on the computer so that the older woman could someday publish her "remembrances."

The "cowboys" stopped singing a range ditty when she came downstairs with Zip and Slide. The greyhounds padded by her side as she walked by Evan, who was sprawled in a chair, his boots up on the table and his shirt opened to his waist. The long gingham ruffle, which she intended to sew on a new curtain, curled around his head and his throat to lend a debonair look. He lifted his mug of foamy beer to her, then higher to toast Miss Matilda.

Clementine lifted her nose and swept by him.

It occurred to her that neither James nor Morris had drawn the intense reaction Evan could with one quick hungry look. While they hadn't scored well on the "Profile of a Lover" test, Evan had definitely shown promise. Morris and James also had not scored well in the tests for attractive male, sizzling looks or heartthrob sections. Neither of them would have cared about an old mule with aching legs or a descented skunk or a boy who desperately needed a father's attention. Though Evan's heart was layered with scars, he was a kind, thoughtful man.

She wanted everything from Evan, and while she was a sharing, giving person, she refused to share him or his toasts with Matilda.... The thought of another woman tasting Evan's belly button caused her to glare at him on her way back from the kitchen.

He blew her a gallant, elegant kiss and grinned boyishly, which sent happy little tingles up her spine. It was then that Clementine decided that Evan wore gingham well and looked quite edible in ruffles.

Nine

"There was no need to tell Michael to 'back off,'" Clementine stated when Evan returned from delivering the guests to the tour bus in Loomis. Since it was late Saturday afternoon and the next guests were due to arrive Sunday night, Cookie had decided to look for more recipes and visit her relatives. The June sun slanted through the row of kitchen windows, one of which had new ruffled curtains. The rest waited to be covered.

Clementine continued straightening the new curtains over the kitchen window while Evan stacked groceries on the table and sorted the mail. His gaze slowly took in her bare feet and rose just as slowly up her legs to the knot that tied her blouse under her breasts. Then he tipped back his hat and stood, long legs apart. "Okay, boss," he said too easily.

Clementine stepped up on the chair she was using to hang the curtains. Evan could unnerve her with that clas-

sic western stance—it was absolutely erotic and challeng-
ingly male. With men like Evan around, no wonder Miss
Matilda had that inviting look in her eye.

"Hand me those, please," she said, nodding to the
gingham mound of ruffles spilling across the table. Evan
looked at the cloth as if it might bite him, then crushed it
in one hand and walked toward her. She took a panel and
slid it through the rod, adjusting the folds before she took
its mate from Evan's hand. His other hand strangled another set of curtains.

She slanted a pointed look at him. "I'm a woman of
experience, Evan. Michael was just testing my receptive-
ness to his advances. He wasn't seriously considering
having a romantic encounter with me. We both knew he
was playing games. You frightened him when you appeared from nowhere and glared down at him like an
avenging—gunfighter. You terrified him."

"Uh-huh. He had his hand on your... chest."

"Exactly. My chest... and he was using his fingertips," she corrected. "He was just brushing off some
hay."

"Sure. Uh-huh. Try another one. The guy is a playboy. He had to come here or get cut out of his father's
will. He's in a messy three-wayer. He's so steamed up, he
even made a pass at Cookie. In another minute, he would
have had you down in the hay playing doctor." Evan
scowled at the ruffled curtains in his hand and said tightly,
"He'd probably try... foreplay."

She stared at his determined frown and tightened her
lips. "His scores on the 'Men Demonstrating Emotion'
quiz were great. *He* admitted to crying when he was jilted.
You're still sulking because he scored high on the 'Profile of a Lover' test at the last campfire."

Evan looked up at her, studied her set face, then jerked off his hat and tossed it to the table with the curtains, the groceries and the mail. He placed his hands on his hips, his weight shifted to one long leg. "Just what do you mean, Clementine? I'm not in the mood for a rehash of that sexual dysfunction business."

She flushed and stepped down from the chair, retrieved her curtains and returned to the chair. She ignored him, stepping up to slide the rods through the curtains. She decided to distract him. "I've started placing a percentage of our profit into the fund for the boys' ranch. Boys' *and* girls' ranch," she corrected.

Something made her say what was swirling in her mind. "It's bad enough when you call me 'boss,' giving the guests the impression that you're my hired hand. This is your venture, too, Evan, and it is as much your land as it is mine. I'm not going to leave, nor am I going to sell my share. You'll have to trust me, Evan. Just as I trust you. Trust is very, very important between partners—"

Trust is essential between lovers, she finished mentally, then forced herself to serve her planned discussion of the moment. The next shipment of men would make private conversation impossible. "When the next guests arrive, I won't have you lurking around—"

Evan's eyebrows lifted. "Lurking?"

She turned away from him, veiling her flush. "While you're not into showing your emotions—and I happen to know that you are a very, very emotional man, Evan . . . you acted as if you . . . as if you and I . . . were—"

"We haven't for a while, Clementine," Evan stated huskily and the chair beneath Clementine's bare feet seemed to wobble unsteadily. She curled her toes into the oak seat of the chair and briskly arranged the gathers on the curtain rods. She breathed lightly, realizing that the room was suddenly very still and warm. Her body tensed and her heart raced.

As she stood on the chair, her back to him, Evan's hands closed gently around her waist, squeezed slightly, then slid to her hips. ''I miss you, Clementine Rose,'' he said simply, that deep raw quality of his voice reaching inside to snare her heart.

She trembled slightly. She truly missed Evan. But she was set on her course and she wanted the matter resolved before the next guests arrived. She was afraid to turn to him, afraid that he would see her expression of longing. Her fingers fluttered over the curtains and stopped suddenly when Evan's hands tightened on her hips, a gentle claiming. ''I know you're recovering from Claudia's jilting of you . . . you could be on the rebound.''

Clementine closed her eyes and prayed that the only rebound Evan thought about was in basketball terms.

''Mmm . . . confused . . . rebound . . . Celtics . . . Lakers . . . Bulls,'' Evan repeated in a distracted, husky tone. His mention of professional basketball teams encouraged Clementine and satisfied her fears. A happy little zing went through her. She tried word association again. ''Cinnamon,'' she said.

''Mmm . . . spice . . . sweet . . . you . . .''

She swallowed and pressed her luck. Evan loved her apple dumplings. ''Apple dumplings,'' she found herself saying in a quivering voice.

''Mmm,'' he murmured appreciatively.

She shivered again as his hands slid higher to press gently into her waist. Her fingers clutched the curtain rod for a lifeline in her swaying, heating emotions. Clementine swallowed, determined to continue with her thoughts while her impulses told her to test Evan's response to the word *love*. "You're adjusting to our partnership... sharing decisions very well— although you remain a bit stubborn on the issue of a girls' ranch. But I think you're making progress—"

"Mmm... that's good... progress...."

Evan's nibbling and kissing the backs of her knees caused Clementine to stop thinking. She placed both hands on the rod now and clung to it while Evan's kisses trailed higher on the back of her left thigh, then on her right one.

Clementine stepped briskly down from the chair and moved to the kitchen counter to slice the fresh lemon meringue pie that she had just made. She inhaled as Evan's body warmed her back and his hands came slowly around her waist, his fingers caressing her. One calloused hand slid under her shorts and rubbed her stomach, which she sucked in. He nuzzled the back of her ear, the side of her throat and Clementine tried desperately to remember her train of thought. "We... ah... seem to be working well together... but... ah... you mustn't confuse issues."

His warm breath swirled around and into her ear and she gripped the counter for support. "Issues?"

"If you can just open up—tell me what you're feeling—I can better analyze..." The last word rose high and quivered in the sunlit kitchen as Evan's large hands claimed her breasts.

"Apple dumplings," he murmured in a delicious, hungry tone.

Clementine's body clenched as he luxuriously caressed her breasts. Evan had skipped back to the word associations. She tried to find the association between her body and the desserts and failed. "Ah... I think I found a test that will pinpoint your exact reluctance to—"

"Turn around and kiss me like you did behind the chuck wagon, Clemmie," Evan ordered in a low, tense tone that ran up the back of her neck and poured through her body like warm, dark silk. There was a fierce desperation in his deep voice that matched the need within her. "Kiss me like you belong to me and you want me more than you wanted anyone in your life."

"Is that how you feel?" she asked shakily, wavering in her determination to push on with her attempt to rescue Evan.

"Uh-huh. You're a sweet, loving woman, Clementine Rose," Evan whispered rawly. "Thank you for that day."

Clementine's resolve to make headway in getting Evan to reveal his emotions slid to the boards of the kitchen floor. She knew he was referring to their lovemaking at the cabin. She turned slowly in his arms and looked up to read the question in his eyes. She knew then—she loved him deeply.

She loved him. Every part of her belonged to Evan Tanner and only him. She touched his high cheekbones, the tiny scar on his jaw, and his firm, sensuous mouth, which opened to suck her fingertip inside, nibbling on it as he watched her expression. She saw him as a gentle, caring man...a man who saw others' fears and weaknesses and who helped when he could...a man who struggled with the coldness and scars inside his heart and who listened to a troubled, needing teen. The slight tremor in his hands and the wary smoky gaze beneath his dark lashes told her that he cared, that he wanted her and what lay inside her—who she would be when the years settled upon her.

"Do you have your harmonica?" she managed to say through the emotions storming her.

"Back pocket. I played a bit on the trail coming back here. You don't want lessons now, do you?" he asked, frowning.

Clementine wrapped her arms around his neck and stood on tiptoe to whisper against his lips. "You are going to serenade me, Evan Tanner. Because you play with your soul and I need to hear what is in your heart and mind tonight. Take me upstairs," she said very quietly before he lifted her into his arms.

"Okay, boss," he murmured softly against her lips. As he carried her slowly up the stairs, Clementine snuggled to him, trembling a bit for what was to come.

Evan kissed and warmed each portion of her body as he drew away her clothing and eased her to the old bed. It creaked gently as if welcoming them. On her way onto the mattress and while watching the dark fires in his eyes, Clementine promised herself that Evan would never think of Miss Matilda Dryer in the same way again.

He loved her so well, she forgot about hearing his soulful harmonica.

The music Evan created that night was long and sweet and tender. It was so magically intense that once, Clementine gripped the bars on the old bed with all her might, afraid that she would shatter into bits of heat and lightning.

Which she did.

Evan stood at the window, staring out into the gray light preceding the dawn. Clementine lay snuggled under the blankets on the old bed that had creaked gently through the night as they made love.

She was changing him, replacing the shadows and bringing back the memories trimmed of their pain.

Ben Tanner had taught him how to play the old songs on the harmonica, giving him a heritage that he hoped to share with the boys he wanted so desperately to help. Ranching stories passed on from his grandfather, through his father, flitted through Evan's memories— The old-time righteousness of revenge of a mean man's horse and a woman who took her shiftless husband to work in the family buggy and left him; the best way to settle down bees while taking their honey; how to stretch an animal hide.... Evan remembered his father boasting about the first time "my boy" rode a half-wild Appaloosa stallion.

The light shifted on Clementine's hippopotamuses and their tutus and Evan was drawn back to the bed and the woman whom he feared he would hurt. She deserved love, more than he could give her.

"...Everything...I want everything...."

He didn't have anything to offer her—she already owned the land a man would want to give his lady. Clementine was an emotional, giving woman, while he preferred to keep his heart safe. Evan walked to stand beside the bed, then eased into it, gathering Clementine into his arms. She burrowed against him, snaring him in her arms and legs. Her familiar cinnamony and feminine scents swirled around him, welcoming him home. "Mmm... Buddy-Bear," she murmured, her fingers prowling through the hair on his chest.

Though he recognized a whimsical need to have her whisper an endearment—darling, sweetheart, honey— Evan smiled slowly as the old hotel creaked with sensual whispers of long ago. Her breasts rubbed his ribs enticingly and Evan found himself grinning into the dawn. A man could get used to creaking old beds and sweet-hearted women who wore red boots. He could grow to appreciate hippopotamuses wearing tutus, geraniums growing in porch commodes and ruffled gingham curtains. He inhaled the sweet scents, wallowing in them, and nuzzled Clementine's hair as the dawn rose and spread into the room.

A wonderful new day was coming. He looked forward to it and serving Clementine breakfast in bed—one of the questions in her "Profile of a Lover" test. If he kept working at it, he could raise his scores. This time when he'd made love to Clementine, he'd managed to take off his boots and his jeans, and making love on the bed eased the raw guilt of having taken her on the old cabin floor.

A new day, he thought drowsily, shifting his thigh lazily and enjoying the soft slide of Clementine's against his skin. This Tanner-Barlow partnership might work out, after all.

Not long after he drifted happily off to sleep, Evan awoke tangled in a nightmare of crossword puzzles lacking the final word and failed magazine quizzes that tore Clementine Rose from him. He also recognized the raw sounds of a revving engine.

He gripped her tighter, refusing to release her to the nightmare and his low scores on the "Profile of a Lover" test; she protested in a sleepy sigh, and awake now, Evan realized the cold sweat of fear had bloomed on his upper lip. He realized that the sound of an engine was real and listened carefully. The vehicle was near the old shed.

Minutes later, Evan stood outside near the old shed and listened to the fading sounds of an all-terrain vehicle. The tire tracks matched those near the Tanner cabin. He'd interrupted the tall, slightly built culprit who was dressed in a hooded coat and sunglasses. The neon-pink shoelaces—in worn, but expensive running shoes—had caught the dim light as the vehicle sped away. Evan wound a rope around his hand, then tossed it aside. Whoever had tied the rope around the supporting post of the old shed's porch intended more mischief and Evan would catch him next time.

Without his boots and wearing only his shorts, Evan gingerly picked his way across the ranch yard. He grimly refused to let the troublemaker interrupt his closeness with Clementine and the way he planned to serve her breakfast, right down to the freshly picked bouquet of roses.

When his bare heel struck a pebble, Evan determinedly gritted his teeth and hopped on his way to the hotel. Whoever had intruded into his first all-night, wake-up-to-the-dawn, lovemaking-test-score-raising session with Clementine Rose had a debt to pay.

While he didn't know if he could offer love, he was determined to give Clementine what she wanted, what she deserved, and he vowed that the minute he could spend time with her quizzes, he'd take notes and study them. Clementine deserved whatever made her happy. On his way into the kitchen to start her breakfast, Evan stopped by Clementine's new herb starts. He read the vitamin instructions and mixed the drops with the proper amount of water in the bottle. He misted her plants and studied the gingham curtains she had made.

They suited him just fine.

A half hour later, Evan balanced the tray in his hands and eased the door to the upstairs room closed. He stealthily turned the key in the old brass lock—he had plans to continue raising his scores on Clementine's magazine quizzes. He smiled briefly at the roses that had burst into magnificent, huge blooms with regular doses of Clementine's garden "tea," a manure and water mixture. A true romantic, she liked to think of bygone ladies of the night lazing in the beautiful old garden.

Evan liked to think of Clementine lazing in bed, snugly warm and rosy from making love with him. He considered her bare shoulder gleaming creamily in the dim light and hoped that Cookie would take her time digging out prime no-lard recipes. The new busload of would-be cowboys was due in Loomis at three o'clock that afternoon. Evan counted the precious minutes alone with Clementine and wished for another week, another month of waking up to her. He placed the tray filled with coffee, orange juice and whole-grain cereal on the bedside table and slid into bed to cuddle Clementine.

She awoke suddenly, bumped his chin on her way to sitting up and jerked the quilt to her chest. She leaned against the old bed's bars, the ones she had gripped several times during the night.

Evan rubbed his chin and wished he'd taken time to shave as he noted the tiny chafe marks on Clementine's throat, which was turning an interesting shade of pink.

He studied her and she looked back at him.

"I've never stayed all night in a woman's bed since my divorce," Evan admitted baldly, the admission stinging him. "Do you want me to leave?"

She blinked sleepily, pushed a strand of hair from her hot cheek and stated huskily, "I'm naked under the quilt, Evan. I have never slept naked—buck-naked, as you say— in my entire life." She studied him. "Your hair stands out in peaks—it's delightful," she exclaimed as though unwrapping a brand-new, very special present. "Evan, your beard glistens."

Then she studied the length and shape of his body beneath the light covering. "You're...ah...you must be naked, too."

Evan felt like laughing outright for joy; he settled for a grin and a western "Yep. Reckon so."

She issued a very small "Oh," and Evan noted the soft fullness of her lips. "I'm glad," he said simply, bending to nuzzle under the quilt and kiss her bare shoulder. "I made breakfast for us."

She blinked, blowing a wayward tendril from her lips. "You know, Evan, I thought I heard a car out in the yard this morning. Was anyone here? Did I dream it, or did you leave— You did? You made breakfast for me?"

While Evan wanted to protect her from worry about the mischief problem, he preened a bit mentally under the happy surprise in her voice; he'd scored higher on the "Profile of a Lover." "Yep. Sure did."

Clementine studied him, their discarded clothing strewn on the furniture and around the room. "We weren't very neat."

"Sometimes neatness counts. Sometimes other things are more important," he returned and prayed that Clementine wasn't regretting the night. He waited tensely for her reaction to him sharing her bed.

Then she grinned at him, and snuggled closer. The tightness in Evan's throat eased and he realized he'd been holding his breath. "What did you cook for me?" she asked with a grin that died when he lifted the tray onto the bed.

Tears came to her eyes as she ran her fingertip across the dewy petals of the pink, yellow and red brilliant, huge roses.

The sunlight flowing into the room caught on a single, shimmering tear as it slid from her lashes to plop on Evan's bare chest. Just for a moment, he thought the sunlight and the joy had seeped through to his heart, easing and warming it. Emotions swirled around him and he felt very fragile. "Oh, Clementine Rose," he whispered unevenly, tilting her chin up for his light kiss.

He didn't mind her hugging him then. Or what followed later.

Making love to Clementine on a bed splashed with sunlight and rose petals was a beautiful, reverent memory that Evan intended to repeat.

The next guests arrived late that afternoon, and for the next two weeks, Evan, Clementine and Cookie worked to make their stay a success. There was little time for deepening their relationship, other than a quick kiss over the computer or snuggling in the pantry.

Cookie's yodeling warned them of her whereabouts in the hotel and Evan spent hours on his bedroll thinking about Buddy-Bear's luck and the old bedsprings creaking and Clementine holding him tight. He also thought about his father and the frustration that dying laid on him.

Because he wanted to please Clementine, Miss Matilda Dryer was tucked in the dry tack room, her curves draped with a layer of protective covering. Evan was especially careful not to enter the hotel at night—he didn't want the other men getting ideas that could gain them bruises. Cookie began rocking her chair on the front porch, and the light in the hotel's windows showed Clementine moving around in the old saloon. When Evan noted the scent of fresh paint, Cookie appeared the next day with four empty tin cans. The dark red paint was to be the background for the new primitive painting class she was taking by mail. Clementine's eyes widened when he offered to carry out the old Bliss hotel sign, which was covered with a tarp. "I'm using it to paint on, Evan," Cookie informed him after popping her latest, biggest bubble yet. "Keeps the paint from getting on the floor."

Brent discovered a "Go for it" in hot-pink sprayed on the root-cellar door and quickly covered the words with a dark brown shade. "I'll spend more time on the lookout," he said as Evan frowned at the wooden door. "Cookie knows. She likes me keeping an eye out for the troublemaker. I could stay overnight and go on the roundup. I'm good with ranch work."

Evan tipped back his hat and regarded the boy whose gaze shifted away. "Your dad needs you, Brent. You're welcome here and I appreciate your time watching out for us—but maybe you'd better spend a little time at home, right?"

Brent bristled slightly. "My dad doesn't have time for me. He's always making big deals. He doesn't need me." Then he was walking off to help Clementine adjust the garden sprinkler. She grinned at him and said something, then Brent ran for the faucet to turn the water on full blast. Clementine pointed the hose at the new corn and Evan, laughing delightedly when he yelled and picked up a bucket of water to throw at her.

While they stood in the garden and grinned at each other, Brent called, "Hey, you guys, next time use squirt guns. You got me wet."

The Fourth of July holiday weekend spread over the Barlow Guest Ranch with a beautiful sweet calm. Cookie had gone to Seattle to tape a talk show with her publisher concerning her pioneer no-lard cookbook. Clementine would have five glorious days alone with Evan. She intended to use every moment, and by the end of the time, he would know how much she loved him.

From her experience in analyzing people with tests, she knew that Evan was very fragile; he had to be handled delicately. She intended to ease into the subject of love, allowing him to open up to her about his deepest, truest feelings about her.

His lovemaking reflected tenderness and passion and his scores had definitely improved in the friend and lover department. She awoke smiling, curled "buck-naked" against Evan in the bedroll in a pine-sheltered glade. The idea to leave Zip and Slide with Brent at the hotel was a good one—the cowards were frightened by deer, which now passed the camp on their way to water at the creek. Brent had also offered to answer the telephone and frighten the rabbits away from her new crop of lettuce. She listened to the rippling stream, the forest awakening and the steady, slow beat of Evan's heart. She wanted to wake up beside him for the rest of her life.

The idea to camp was Evan's idea, a marvelous one. They camped on the bank of the stream where Evan would show her how to fish, where his father had taken him as a boy. The ride from the hotel was romantic, Evan holding her against him as Yuma walked through the sage brushed with the golden sunset. Mosey followed, packed with a minimum of camping gear and Pow-Wow carried the tiny portable toilet at Clementine's insistence. Evan cooked dinner, grilled fish that he had caught before he'd come to claim her, campfire-baked potatoes and roast corn. Her apple dumplings topped off the meal and set Evan foraging for other cinnamony confections.

Then they had lain beneath the stars, a slow, quiet time.

Now Evan's heart began to beat faster and his hand tightened on her hip. "People sometimes wake up with rattlesnakes on their bedrolls—they seek the heat," he said sleepily as he stretched.

She crowded closer to him in the predawn. "Evan, do something," she whispered urgently.

"Oh, I plan to," he said huskily and he gently lifted himself over her.

Ten

"We have to get married," Evan stated in a raspy, uneven tone as he braced his weight away from her. The passionate moments they had just shared had melted Clementine's very bones into a liquid happiness; in her heavenly condition, Evan's deep, breathless voice seemed very distant. Though Evan hadn't played his harmonica for her alone, there was other more intimate music—like the smoky hunger of his eyes and the trembling sweep of his hand claiming her—that she knew came from his heart.

At the very height of her passion—or was it when she was floating down to the safety of Evan's arms?—she had whispered her love. Since Evan had just issued a soul-filled shout, she doubted that he had heard her. She would tell him gently when his heartbeat slowed from the galloping rhythm of the current moment.

Evan was a caring lover, drawing every emotion from her and responding magnificently to her almost shameful, hussylike hunger for him.

Clementine stirred beneath him now, pleasantly sated. She smoothed the muscles on his back and they quivered nicely beneath her touch. She ran her hands down his spine and over his hard bottom and patted him affectionately as she had been wanting to do; she was still too shy with him to enter any serious belly-button nuzzling. Evan kissed her swollen, tender lips and eased his head down to lie beside hers. "Clemmie, are you awake?"

She noted the smile in his voice, as though he was quite satisfied with himself. He moved on her luxuriously, as though settling into a lifetime with her. The thought pleased her—a lifetime of Evan. "Don't try that rattle-snake gimmick again," she murmured, biting his ear gently. "It won't work a second time."

Evan's smile curved against her throat, his beard slightly rasping her heated skin. "Let's get married," he whispered.

Clementine's eyes opened to the shadowy pine trees in the early dawn. She eased gently away from him, which was difficult in the bedroll. Evan placed his open hand on her stomach and massaged it gently, reminding her of the deep need she experienced at the very height of their passion—when Evan was giving himself to her, she desperately wanted his children. "Well?" he asked, prompting her as a mourning dove began to coo. "What do you think?"

She thought she wanted a very necessary admission of love from the man lying intimately against her, his hand caressing her gently. There was a big gap between *having* to get married and *wanting* to share happiness, lives and love.

Clementine decided to sort through her unraveling emotions before saying anything. She pushed back the slight fizz of anger welling up from her innermost depths. Unused to opening his heart, perhaps Evan needed coaching. "Why?" she asked with every particle of her body tightening, her stomach contracting in a painful knot.

He brushed back a tendril from her lips and kissed them gently, then braced his head on his hand. "We're a good mix. Like mules pulling in harness," he said thoughtfully.

Her heavenly condition chipped a bit, but Clementine was determined to help Evan open his heart. "Go on."

"I don't like the gossip about us that's sure to come, Clemmie," he stated grimly. "It's not good for business."

She swallowed, her heart beating wildly. "Business?"

Oh, Evan...Evan...do you love me...? Please say something right, she coached mentally.

He inhaled abruptly and his eyes flicked to deer passing the sumac stand. He watched as they slid down to the creek and began watering, despite Mosey's braying protest. "I can take all that bull about the hired hand marrying above himself to get the business, the Tanner land—because it isn't true. What's between you and me doesn't include the Tanners and the Barlows."

Oh, please, Evan...please say you love me....

He frowned at the deer. "I won't say I agree with you about the girls' ranch or make any promises other than I'll take care of you the best way I know how."

"An arrangement just like the one you wanted with Claudia?" Clementine asked very carefully. "The old sister-switch?"

His frown jerked down to her. "We've got something a little bit different from my relationship with Claudia—like the heat running between us and the lovemaking. I never made love to Claudia," he stated firmly. "But we're a good balance—at first I didn't think our partnership would work, but now I do."

She flushed when she thought of the "something a little different." Clementine squirmed from the bedroll and tugged on Evan's shirt, buttoning it with trembling fingers. "If you think that we...that I..." She motioned to the bedroll they had shared. "If you think that I would accept marriage without love, you can think again, Evan Tanner...Mr. Romance."

"What's love got to do with it?" Evan flipped back the bedroll and stood on it, his tall, nude body reminding her of how well she had just been loved. She forced her eyes to stay above his shoulders.

He tilted his head determinedly, the peaks of his hair still standing out from her fingers. Her flush deepened as she remembered how she had tugged his lips to hers, how she had held his head to her breasts, crying out with the tenderness of his loving. "A business relationship—is that how you see it?" she demanded shakily as she bent to tug on her red boots.

Evan placed his hands on his hips. "A pretty damn fine one, I'd say. I don't want gossip interfering with business."

Clementine tossed out her hands and fought tears. "Oh, sure. Business is good. The partnership is working out. We don't want gossip interfering with business, do we? Oh, that's a wonderful reason to marry, Evan."

"You're getting het up—riled—Clementine," Evan warned ominously.

She straightened, threw up her hands and muttered, "I am more than 'het up,' Mr. Business-and-Bed."

"It's not like that," he stated flatly, the tiny vein throbbing in his temple. "We're good together. The fresh garden vegetables and the apple dumplings as a house specialty were great additions. Cookie's cookbook and the other things you've suggested will make good take-home gifts—"

He stopped talking and grabbed his boot, which Clementine had just hurled at him. His mouth tightened as he caught the second boot. "That's a fine way for a lady to act when a man tells her they should get married—Anything else you'd like to throw at me?" he asked too politely.

"I never lose my temper, Evan Tanner. But you are enough to test the most patient person—which I am... which I have always been, until meeting you," she informed him tightly, then began running in the direction of the hotel. Evan's shirt fluttered around her bare thighs and she pushed the long, dangling shirtsleeve up to dry her tear-stained face.

Mosey ignored Evan's command to stop and brayed his sympathies. He and Pow-Wow followed her as she crossed the field on her way to the hotel. Daisy looked at her and Clementine stopped to hug the small cow like a dear, safe friend in a slashing, dangerous hurricane.

Because she didn't want to spend the day amid the whispers of the hotel's shady, sizzling past and within sight of the bed where Evan had made love to her, Clementine rode Belle into Loomis. She visited the monuments to the great Native American chiefs who had helped the settlers, then stopped to visit Cookie's friend, Pecos, for "no-lard" apple pie and coffee. When Mosey appeared at Pecos's door, Clementine decided to purchase bing cherries and an assortment of fresh fruit for making jams. On the way back to the ranch, she leisurely picked blackberries with Nelda, a Nez Perce neighbor. Clementine tried not to think of how many times James and Morris had told her they loved her and how Evan hadn't once mentioned the emotion.

He wanted a business marriage...to stop gossip... "two mules in harness."...

Clementine didn't want to be compared to a mule, no matter how much she loved Mosey. James and Morris had hurt her, but nothing like the emotions that ran through her when she realized the depth—rather the lack of depth—of Evan's proposal of marriage.

His missing statement of love was like the last word on his crossword puzzles. They wouldn't be complete without it. Clementine realized that *she* would probably feel like an unfinished crossword puzzle for the rest of her life.... Pain clenched her heart.

Actually, with very little trouble, Evan had substituted her for Claudia. The old sister-switch, she repeated mentally.

Evan was waiting for her when she returned to the hotel laden with "jam makings."

His mood hadn't improved as he unloaded the mules and unsaddled Belle. Minutes later, he walked into the kitchen where she was scrubbing jars furiously. "I want this out," he said flatly, tossing his hat to the table.

She didn't turn from the sink. Until she could think clearly, she didn't want to discuss Evan's proposed loveless arrangement. "I'm making jam this weekend, Evan. Sorry...no time to talk."

"Lady, this morning you tromped across that field like a mad hornet."

"Yes...well, I may just tromp back across it," she returned hotly, walking past him into the saloon. She pressed her lips together, resenting that only Evan could draw her anger surging from her.

"Better not. Better stay put until we hash this out," Evan warned in a deadly tone behind her. She stopped in midstride. While she had intended to pick up the fruit baskets and carry them into the kitchen, his tone challenged her.

If she was in the mood for anything, it was meeting Evan's challenges. She turned to him. "You can't run me off or make me stay put by threats, Evan Tanner."

Across the looming shadows of the saloon, Evan leveled a stare at her. She stared back and knew that she had never been more angry or hurt in her life. "I asked you to marry me," he stated.

"It wasn't a question—will I or won't I. It was your statement that we should get married...a comfortable business arrangement and all, you know—"

The door opened and Brent walked into the room with Zip and Slide at his heels. Clementine noted distantly that Brent's shoelaces were a neon pink. The youth's smile died as he looked at Evan and Clementine. Then he said, "Hey, Evan, I found the saddle in that old shack down by the creek. It's okay."

"Good," Evan said tightly, holding Clementine's gaze with his dark, stormy one.

"What saddle?" Clementine asked.

Brent shifted restlessly, looking to Evan for guidance. The two males looked at each with an understanding that deepened Clementine's unfamiliar anger; clearly, Evan warned him not to say more. Evan ran his hand through his hair. "One has been missing. Thanks for locating it, Brent."

Clementine stiffened and realized that her eyebrow had been quivering. "A saddle has been missing and no one told me?" she asked in a high, tight tone.

"Don't get riled up," Evan murmured after a long pause in which he studied her eyebrows.

"'Riled up' is too mild for how I feel, Mr. Tanner," Clementine stated. She looked down at the table where Evan had evidently been working crossword puzzles while he waited for her. One glance at the last empty space and a riveting pain shot through her. She jabbed her index finger to the empty word blocks. "Trust."

"Ah...maybe I'd better go," Brent said warily as Evan and Clementine continued to stare at each other.

"You stay," she ordered, then walked to the tarp covering the old Bliss Hotel and Saloon sign. "You may as well see this."

She pulled away the tarp; it fell from her hands. She looked at the sign she had carefully restored every evening while Cookie kept watch on the porch. The dark red, turn-of-the-century-style lettering had taken her hours; she had relished revealing the sign to Evan and announcing her decision. The scrolling Barlow-Tanner Ranch letters were ruined now, splashed by white paint that she had used on the background.

Behind her, Evan's voice was low and angry. "What's that supposed to mean?"

Clementine closed her eyes; her nails bit into her palms. Suddenly, she felt very old and tired. The sign looked as ruined as her hopes that Evan loved her. "We've had trouble at the ranch before, haven't we? You told Brent and probably Cookie, too, not to bother me with it. You didn't think I could handle problems and you didn't share them with me." *Just as you won't share your heart,* she finished mentally. "You didn't trust me to cope with problems, Evan. You *don't* trust me," she corrected achingly.

She fought tears, hating the one that spilled over her lashes and down her cheek, as she asked, "Did you think I wouldn't notice the lack of love and trust?"

"Clementine . . ." Evan's voice was wistful as his large hands closed over her shoulders.

She moved away from him, feeling as though she were unraveling into a pool of unmatched, tangled threads. The bright pink, happy thread meant she loved Evan deeply and knew that he cared for her—the shocking red thread was the passion they had shared. Was it only empty passion that Evan felt? Did he somewhere in his deepest heart love her?

Then the ugly black thread snared around her ankles—his lack of trust in her and the secrets that yawned before her. She was too tired to deal with any more heartbreaks today. "The sign was a surprise for you. I wanted our partnership to be even—fifty-fifty. I think Dad would have wanted it that way. He always liked your father and you, Evan. . . . He'd been holding the land until you came back and was thrilled the day you proposed the guest ranch. By that time, he knew his heart wouldn't last much longer. He said you were an honorable man who valued family and land and he wanted you here, on your family land . . . he said Ben Tanner was the best man he'd ever known and that you were like him. . . . I'm going upstairs now. It's been a long day. . . ."

Then she paused and gripped the banister. "You were right, after all . . . I'm not staying. . . . You can have the ranch."

Clementine moved slowly up the stairs, her hand using the hand railing for support. Zip and Slide glided quietly at her heels as if sensing their mistress's bleak mood. Evan remembered the happy way she had slid down the wood railing. A stark, raw jolt of pain tore through him, ripping away the beauty he had felt in the past few days. The startling dream of waking up to Clementine's smile this morning shimmered in front of him and evaporated. He couldn't move; the nightmare of her running across the meadow, running from him, caught him just as it had then.

He shivered with the shadows and the cold seeping into him, despite the warm July evening. He touched her beret lying on the table next to his crossword puzzle. His father had once said that a loving woman needed a loving man . . . he'd also said that sometimes a man couldn't let go of the darkness and give the woman the love she needed and that was "an awful, lonesome shame." Then Evan glanced at the sign, carefully repainted by Clementine—her gift to him.

What did he know about loving? What made him think that he could love her in the way she deserved to be loved?

Evan looked down at Brent's neon-pink shoelaces and inhaled slowly. He had a long night ahead of him, searching the emotions he'd kept buried for so many years. With every ounce of his being, he would find what lay between Clementine and himself...because he wanted her and he wanted her happiness. The loving feeling inside him might not be deep enough, or true enough to give Clementine what she needed.

Evan straightened his shoulders. He'd made a mess of his chance with Clementine and he intended to bridge the gap between them. There had been more than business on his mind when he'd mentioned marriage—more like an everyday loving feeling and babies and the feeling that they were walking on sunbeams and clover. More like

growing old with her and loving the way she smelled—
Evan grimaced. Oh, no, he hadn't said any of that—
Whatever happened between them tomorrow morning, he
had a task at hand that couldn't wait any longer. "Brent,
let's take a ride out to the old cabin. There's something
I've been wanting to discuss with you."

"This place is creepy," Brent said later in the cabin as
Evan tugged the old footlocker into the center of the
room. He sat on it and looked at the spot where he had
taken Clementine.

Making love to her was as natural and sweet as honey,
as hot as a forest fire sweeping across the tops of the pines.
He'd come home that day, really home, to the part of him
that had been missing, and he'd fight not to lose her.

"Sit down, Brent. Let's spend a while here. I'm sort-
ing out some things and you can, too. You can start by
telling me if I can look forward to any other mischief."

Brent's eyes widened and he swallowed, his Adam's
apple bobbing on his thin throat. His gangling frame
shifted on the old wooden apple box. "What do you
mean?"

"You're lonely, Brent. So you created trouble, then
offered to help. That way, you thought you could spend
more time with us. You remind me of myself back when I
was your age, except you've got some money and times
were pretty tough when I was growing up. You come over
as often as you want. You didn't need to pull those
pranks—pushing over the outhouse and stealing the saddle."

Brent's face darkened. "Who says I did it?"

"Me," Evan returned gently. He looked around the
cobwebs and the dust. "You know, I grew up here. My
dad died here, a bitter old man. We just rumbled around

in this little cabin, two lonesome people. I resented him dying, and he hated it, too.''

"Ben Tanner was the best man he'd ever known...." Evan began to realize that his father hadn't known how to express his love, either—but it had been there. Bits and pieces of those hard days came flowing back. "Looking back, I know that he taught me a few things along the way—like how to hunt and track. That's how I know the tire marks of your rig fit the marks on the tires that pulled over the outhouse. You might want to use a cut limb with leaves to brush away tracks next time. Then there are those shoelaces. They're hard to miss.''

Brent looked down at his shoes and inhaled. "I like being at your ranch. You guys have time to talk with me. Even when you're working—you and Clementine and Cookie—you listen or you talk or there's just the feeling that I belong to somebody.''

"Belonging is important." Evan looked out into the evening sky. "There's the North Star.''

"Uh-huh.'' Brent shifted uneasily. "Are you going to report me or tell Dad?''

Evan shrugged. "No. But I want you to spend time thinking about yourself and what you want for yourself—not for today or tomorrow—but what you want when you're my age. About a million years ago, I knew a young guy like you. He didn't think his dad cared, but he did. His father just didn't know how to show it. It cost a big chunk out of that boy's life, before he put the pieces together. Don't make that mistake, Brent. You're a strong person. Remember that when times get tough. You can handle whatever comes. Make a good life for yourself.''

"Nobody talks to me like you do. I just wanted to be around, you know? I'm sorry I caused trouble. I'm sorry about the sign.''

"You're going to repaint that sign, son," Evan stated gently. "And maybe dig a hole for the new outhouse on the north quarter pasture...after you build one. Along the way, we're going to talk about your future. That is, if you can't heal things with your dad. He loves you."

"He's got girlfriends."

"And he's got a son who I know loves him. Talk to him about what you're feeling. Think about it and bring it out in the open. Then call your mother. Talk with her. Sometimes, older people can't take the first step—but someone has to. May as well be you. At least you'll know that you tried hard, and no one can ask more than that. Just try. Let some of what has happened fall away like rain from a good, solid roof. Come over and talk with us— Clementine knows more about this relating business than me, but I'm trying to learn. You're welcome any time, day or night. I'll help, if I can."

"I caused trouble between you and Clementine," Brent insisted. "She'll leave now."

Evan looked up at that first star he saw and made a wish he'd learned as a child. "I'm working on keeping her. She needs a loving man and I haven't had much experience with that. I hurt her."

"Good luck," Brent said in a serious tone. "She's special. I like those silly hugs and kisses. She scared me spitless the first time, but now—uh...now, they're sort of neat. I think...I think maybe I'll try to learn some of that. Men do that stuff now, you know."

"It's a start. I've been thinking about trying some of it myself." The two men looked steadily at each other before Evan nodded and stood. "You'd better go on home now. Take the high trail. It's safer at night. Or you can leave your horse here to graze overnight and take the rig you've hidden in that brush. It has headlamps."

After Brent left, Evan rigged two long poles from Yuma's saddle; they dragged the ground behind the horse and would bear the old footlocker back to the hotel. It was going to be a long night; he owed it to Clementine to tell her his exact feelings. He intended to face her in the morning, before she left him forever, and to do that, he had to know everything about himself.

Clementine awoke to the sound of music, a harmonica playing heart-and-soul music softly in the shadowy dawn. It was old music, the cowboy-sitting-around-campfire music from long ago. A lonely pain rode the sounds, quivering gently in the shadows. She was drained from the sleepless night, afraid to come down into the saloon when she heard movement. She didn't want to face Cookie—if she'd come back early—and she couldn't bear to see Evan just yet.

He was near her now; she caught his familiar scents, inhaling them slowly, wrapping them around her for an eternity—because she knew she'd never love another man as fiercely, as truly as she loved Evan Tanner—the mean-hearted cuss.

She opened her eyes to glare at him as he sat by her bed. "I need my sleep."

The sight of him tore her heart, deep shadows ran beneath his smoky eyes, his unshaven cheeks moving with the breath he used in the harmonica. His hair was rumpled and peaked as though he'd run his fingers through it many times. His shirt was open down the front and his long, jean-covered legs were propped on the foot of her bed, his feet bare and his toes moving to the soul-filled music. Evan watched her, his hands moving the harmonica back and forth, cupping it, blowing and inhaling, and releasing the muted sounds. The music was so beautiful, so lonesome that she wanted to cry—if she didn't want to cry already. She flipped over on her side away from him and stealthily edged up a corner of the light blanket to dry her eyes.

Evan's feet found her bottom, nudging her into a rocking movement that creaked the old bed gently. She knew it was his feet, because he needed two hands for the harmonica and the soulful music hadn't stopped. Clementine swallowed. "Go away."

Then he played an old song she recognized, which used her name, "Clementine." As she fought tears and listened to the mournful song, she remembered that Evan had never called her "his darling." She hoped he didn't hear her sniff. Just those three times.

"Holding you would make this a whole lot easier, Clementine Rose," Evan said huskily. She sensed that he was hesitant—even afraid.

No one had ever accused her of being coldhearted. If Evan was going to tell her he only wanted a business arrangement, she might as well take the pain in this grand old bed, because she surely couldn't move.

"Okay," she whispered shakily, scooting over slightly. So much for her resolve to ignore him, she thought sadly. She expected Evan to lie on top of the light blanket, but instead, he slid under it and his body curled along her back. His toes found hers...the old bed creaked gently beneath them. There was a pause in which Clementine's heart stopped and then Evan's arm came around her waist. His cheek settled gently on hers. He inhaled slowly several times and his arm gathered her closer until she could feel his heart beating rapidly against her back.

He nuzzled her cheek. "You're wearing my shirt."

She'd worn it because it kept him closer to her for just a little longer. His beard scraped her cheek gently as she nodded. They lay quietly, Evan's body curling around hers, his toes moving beneath hers. Then he whispered huskily, wistfully against her ear, "So I guess you're not going to call me sweetheart or honey or any of those other names people in love call each other, hmm?"

She swallowed, shaking her head slightly. She'd wanted to, but then she had been afraid she'd frighten him, and now it was too late. "The bottom line is you don't love me, Evan."

"Who says so?" he returned huskily, his body tensing behind hers. When she didn't answer, Evan kissed her cheek. "I love you, Clementine Rose. I always have, from the first minute I saw you and that ridiculous pancake of a hat and those red boots. I knew I was a goner when you looked at me with those pansy eyes and spouted off that sexual dysfunction business and how you were going to rescue me. But changes take time and I'm learning. Last night, I went through my family's things—remember that old footlocker? It was filled with photographs and letters and my folks' wedding rings. I was too young to see the love between them then. Or the way my father loved me. But last night, I knew for certain. It hurt—opening up the past, things I'd buried away, but I did. Because I do love you, Clementine Rose . . . because what we have is important enough to fight for, even fight the past. . . . I wanted to come to you free of the scars that kept me from telling you that I love you."

"You do?" she heard her high, breathless voice ask.

"Don't talk," he ordered gently, kissing her cheek again. "I've been working on this all night and now you listen, okay?"

She nodded again, her heart doing flip-flops as Evan's hand massaged her stomach and he began to speak, slowly, thoughtfully. "I'm scared now. Afraid of losing you . . . not Tanner land or Barlow land or the business or my dream of having a boys' ranch or the girls' ranch you suggested. You're the other part of me, Clementine. The missing piece of my heart, my soul, the deepest most precious piece. This loving feeling I knew I had for you was really just plain, pure old-fashioned love.''

When he paused, Clementine asked unevenly, "Can I talk now?"

"No. I'm not done," he returned firmly. Then after a pause, he asked shakily against her ear, "Will you marry me, Clementine? Will you marry me because I love you?"

She squeezed her eyes shut, forcing away the tears of pain, making way for the ones of joy. "Can I turn around now?"

"No," he muttered darkly. "One look at you and I can't think. That's part of my problem in dealing with you and this love thing. I look at you and all I can think about is babies and laughter and spending our lives together. I might say the wrong thing. Or not say the right thing. Those hugs and kisses and leg-locks toss away any good sense I've got. We have to practice talking, Clementine. There's so much I want to tell you. No more secrets, Clementine Rose. What would be real nice right now is if you'd give me your answer . . . and pushing my luck, if you'd tell me you loved me like you did when we made love.''

She smiled tremulously, joy spilling out of her heart and to her lips. A quiet, controlled man, Evan's admissions weren't easy for him. Her smile grew as she nuzzled his cheek. "Oh, but darling, I would really like to see your face.''

He considered that for a heartbeat and when he nodded, Clementine wrestled him to his back and lay over him. It was a good feeling, one of coming home. "I love you . . . yes," she whispered against his lips. "Yes."

She kissed the tear on his cheek.

It tasted like forever.

"Now call me honey and sweetheart," he ordered in an uneven, husky whisper as she kissed away another tear.

Epilogue

Clementine paused at the top of the stairs, allowing the train of her French lace bridal gown to be arranged by Claudia and "old S.J." Cookie was sobbing loudly in the saloon while Mark played the electronic piano keyboard. Brent blushed as Clementine slid her hand, clad in a long lace glove, though his elbow. "You look pretty," he whispered.

"You're handsome in a suit." Behind her bridal veil, Clementine fought tears of happiness. Her wedding gown wasn't really recycled—because her love for Evan ran deep and true and new as the dewy, lush red roses that flowed down the banister. Labor Day weekend, the first of September, was a perfect time for a wedding. Evan had stated flatly that he'd have mental damage and real sexual dysfunctioning if he had to wait until the season closed. He had given Brent instructions to block off any trails leading to the ranch the minute the guests left the wedding. He wanted the holiday to be spent with Clementine alone. Brent was to take Zip and Slide home with him.

The wedding march began and the crowd of friends and neighbors turned to look up at her. She inhaled the scent of freshly baked apple dumplings to be served at the reception, and the varied scents of "old S.J.'s" garden-fresh roses of every color filling the hotel.

The huge bouquet of brilliant red roses trembled in Clementine's free hand when her gaze met Evan's. Dressed in a western suit, wearing his Sunday boots, Evan was her future, her life.

She lifted one lace-gloved hand to touch the gold locket he had given her. The antique jewelry had been his mother's and inside rested a picture of Evan grinning rakishly, his hat tipped back as Clementine leg-locked him and waved at the camera. The other side held a picture of Evan's mother and father, young and in love. It was fitting that they attended his wedding, for they had loved him deeply, too.

His gaze followed her down the stairs. She passed the wall filled with framed pictures of his parents and grandparents and her family. Clementine glanced at the brown-tint picture of Evan as a little boy dressed in a too-large cowboy outfit and prayed that one day they would have a son. She moved toward Evan and their marriage with a certainty that their futures would be perfect—as long as they had each other. When Brent gave her hand to Evan, he lifted it to kiss her palm. "I love you," he whispered in the dark, raspy tone that signaled his deepest emotions.

She leaned to kiss him, ignoring the traditional after-the-ceremony schedule.

"I love you, darling," she returned from the depths of her heart. Evan's smoky eyes darkened with pleasure, receiving her pledge and endearment and giving back his own.

Cookie let out a loud wail and began sobbing in earnest, and ready to begin, the minister smiled.

January cloaked the hotel in a fierce winter snowstorm. Mosey, Pow-Wow, Jasmine, Yuma and the other animals were snug in the new barn. Heathcliff wooed his hens while Evan and Clementine settled into their marriage.

Clementine had discovered that Heathcliff's threatening manner was because he was missing ladyloves—she understood what that loss could do to a rooster.

"Okay," Evan agreed thoughtfully, the stub of his thumb stroking his unshaven cheek as he misted water on Jethro and Sissie. Big Bertha moaned seductively in the night as he continued, "I'll teach Maud rope tricks. The brochure is great... and your idea of starting slowly this year with the boys... and girls for alternating holiday weeks during the summer is solid."

"Come here, honey," Clementine invited, snuggling beneath the quilts as the old bed creaked.

Evan quickly placed the water-mist bottle on the table. He hoped Miss Matilda wasn't too lonely in Mark's barn loft. Now when Clementine lay warm and snugly against him, Evan loved to talk quietly about their separate pasts and share the future that would come. He loved to listen to the radio's real deep-down cowboy music with Clementine, when she wasn't analyzing the motivations and the cures. After a heated discussion in which Clementine's eyebrows had quivered, they had settled on listening first, lovemaking second and analyzing lastly. Placing lovemaking first was more the actual order of the list.

"Sweetheart?" Clementine prompted in a sultry way that hastened Evan to the grand old bed. His wife had worried about how the loss of Matilda would affect him and her innovative compensation had stunned Evan at first. After he recovered.

Clementine arched against the trembling caress of Evan's hands, the tender suckling of his lips upon her breasts. She closed her eyes, smoothing the rippling muscles on his back. This gentle man loved her and she sensed that he was tending her carefully, still new with sharing himself with her.

The startling primitive need to be a part of him still frightened her at times. To be locked so closely to Evan that nothing could come between them.

He fitted his mouth over hers and kissed her with his heart and soul, reminding her of the way he played the harmonica just for her. Evan tasted of the cinnamony apple dumplings he loved so much. Occasionally, while they made love, he murmured the strangest comparison between her and apple dumplings.

She'd spent hours looking for a reference in her quiz file; none could be found, although Evan seemed to really enjoy taking her tests—as long as she didn't supply the last words in his crossword puzzles.

The old bed creaked beneath them, and Clementine listened to the familiar, erotic sound, though they had not entered the deepest intimacy. The wind howled around the corners of the old hotel and saloon.... Or was it the sighs of lovemaking long ago?

How she loved this man . . . the way he delighted in loving her . . . in finding ways to open his heart as she opened hers to him.

However, in the last half hour, Evan had been practicing his husbandly-lover-adequate-foreplay techniques so well and so long and so good that Clementine hadn't been able to unlatch her fingers from the old bed's bars.

Because she had a program on her Evan menu, Clementine forced herself to release the bed.

Evan grinned sexily when she managed to wrestle him beneath her. "Clementine Rose, have I told you I love you?" he asked in that husky sound, then his smoky eyes darkened as she smoothed his chest.

Clementine thought of all the mornings she would wake up to this dear, tender, romantic, loving man. She imagined his expression when she would tell him that they had created a new life between them, a child to pass on the Tanner-Barlow heritage.

Then she thought of the more immediate ways she had planned to spend the winter. Evan's eyebrows shot up. "Hey... not now... oh, no, you don't, I'm not up to any serious belly-button nuzzling—not right now. I'm— Do not leg-lock me, Clementine Rose. Or hug me. Not now... not now...."

Sometimes a woman had to do what a woman had to do....

* * * * *

COMING NEXT MONTH

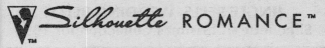

Silhouette ROMANCE™

'Tis the season for romantic bliss.
It all begins with just one kiss—

UNDER THE MISTLETOE

Celebrate the joy of the season and the thrill of romance with this special collection:

Available in December, from Silhouette Romance.

JINGLE BELLS, WEDDING BELLS:
Silhouette's Christmas Collection for 1994

Christmas Wish List

*To beat the crowds at the malls and get the perfect present for *everyone,* even that snoopy Mrs. Smith next door!

*To get through the holiday parties without running my panty hose.

*To bake cookies, decorate the house and serve the perfect Christmas dinner—just like the women in all those magazines.

*To sit down, curl up and read my Silhouette Christmas stories!

Join *New York Times* bestselling author Nora Roberts, along with popular writers Barbara Boswell, Myrna Temte and Elizabeth August, as we celebrate the joys of Christmas—and the magic of marriage—with

$\mathcal{J}$INGLE
BELLS,
$\mathcal{W}$EDDING
BELLS

Silhouette's Christmas Collection for 1994.

Jilted!

Left at the altar, but not for long.

Why are these six couples
who have sworn off love
suddenly hearing wedding bells?

Find out in these scintillating books
by your favorite authors,
coming this November!

#889 **THE ACCIDENTAL BRIDEGROOM**
by Ann Major
(Man of the Month)

#890 **TWO HEARTS, SLIGHTLY USED**
by Dixie Browning

#891 **THE BRIDE SAYS NO**
by Cait London

#892 **SORRY, THE BRIDE HAS ESCAPED**
by Raye Morgan

#893 **A GROOM FOR RED RIDING HOOD**
by Jennifer Greene

#894 **BRIDAL BLUES**
by Cathie Linz

Come join the festivities when six handsome
hunks finally walk down the aisle...

only from

▼ SILHOUETTE®
Desire®

JILT

SILHOUETTE®
Desire®

TWO HEARTS, SLIGHTLY USED
BY DIXIE BROWNING
Book 3 of the OUTER BANKS SERIES!

OUTER BANKS

The way to a Man's Heart Is Through His Stomach!

At least that's what Frances Jones thought—until sexy Brace Ridgeway got the flu and couldn't eat! But by then, Brace only craved a sweet dessert called Frances....

Don't miss
TWO HEARTS, SLIGHTLY USED by Dixie Browning, available in November from Silhouette Desire.

"HOORAY FOR HOLLYWOOD" SWEEPSTAKES

HERE'S HOW THE SWEEPSTAKES WORKS

OFFICIAL RULES — NO PURCHASE NECESSARY

To enter, complete an Official Entry Form or hand print on a 3" x 5" card the words "HOORAY FOR HOLLYWOOD", your name and address and mail your entry in the pre-addressed envelope (if provided) or to: "Hooray for Hollywood" Sweepstakes, P.O. Box 9076, Buffalo, NY 14269-9076 or "Hooray for Hollywood" Sweepstakes, P.O. Box 637, Fort Erie, Ontario L2A 5X3. Entries must be sent via First Class Mail and be received no later than 12/31/94. No liability is assumed for lost, late or misdirected mail.

Winners will be selected in random drawings to be conducted no later than January 31, 1995 from all eligible entries received.

Grand Prize: A 7-day/6-night trip for 2 to Los Angeles, CA including round trip air transportation from commercial airport nearest winner's residence, accommodations at the Regent Beverly Wilshire Hotel, free rental car, and $1,000 spending money. (Approximate prize value which will vary dependent upon winner's residence: $5,400.00 U.S.); 500 Second Prizes: A pair of "Hollywood Star" sunglasses (prize value: $9.95 U.S. each). Winner selection is under the supervision of D.L. Blair, Inc., an independent judging organization, whose decisions are final. Grand Prize travelers must sign and return a release of liability prior to traveling. Trip must be taken by 2/1/96 and is subject to airline schedules and accommodations availability.

Sweepstakes offer is open to residents of the U.S. (except Puerto Rico) and Canada who are 18 years of age or older, except employees and immediate family members of Harlequin Enterprises, Ltd., its affiliates, subsidiaries, and all agencies, entities or persons connected with the use, marketing or conduct of this sweepstakes. All federal, state, provincial, municipal and local laws apply. Offer void wherever prohibited by law. Taxes and/or duties are the sole responsibility of the winners. Any litigation within the province of Quebec respecting the conduct and awarding of prizes may be submitted to the Regie des loteries et courses du Quebec. All prizes will be awarded; winners will be notified by mail. No substitution of prizes are permitted. Odds of winning are dependent upon the number of eligible entries received.

Potential grand prize winner must sign and return an Affidavit of Eligibility within 30 days of notification. In the event of non-compliance within this time period, prize may be awarded to an alternate winner. Prize notification returned as undeliverable may result in the awarding of prize to an alternate winner. By acceptance of their prize, winners consent to use of their names, photographs, or likenesses for purpose of advertising, trade and promotion on behalf of Harlequin Enterprises, Ltd., without further compensation unless prohibited by law. A Canadian winner must correctly answer an arithmetical skill-testing question in order to be awarded the prize.

For a list of winners (available after 2/28/95), send a separate stamped, self-addressed envelope to: Hooray for Hollywood Sweepstakes 3252 Winners, P.O. Box 4200, Blair, NE 68009.

CBSRLS

OFFICIAL ENTRY COUPON

"Hooray for Hollywood"
SWEEPSTAKES!

Yes, I'd love to win the Grand Prize — a vacation in Hollywood —
or one of 500 pairs of "sunglasses of the stars"! Please enter me
in the sweepstakes!

This entry must be received by December 31, 1994.
Winners will be notified by January 31, 1995.

Name _____

Address _____ Apt. _____

City _____

State/Prov. _____ Zip/Postal Code _____

Daytime phone number _____
(area code)

Account # _____

Return entries with invoice in envelope provided. Each book
in this shipment has two entry coupons — and the more
coupons you enter, the better your chances of winning!

DIRCBS

OFFICIAL ENTRY COUPON

"Hooray for Hollywood"
SWEEPSTAKES!

Yes, I'd love to win the Grand Prize — a vacation in Hollywood —
or one of 500 pairs of "sunglasses of the stars"! Please enter me
in the sweepstakes!

This entry must be received by December 31, 1994.
Winners will be notified by January 31, 1995.

Name _____

Address _____ Apt. _____

City _____

State/Prov. _____ Zip/Postal Code _____

Daytime phone number _____
(area code)

Account # _____

Return entries with invoice in envelope provided. Each book
in this shipment has two entry coupons — and the more
coupons you enter, the better your chances of winning!

DIRCBS